GLASS CASTLES

THE RESURRECTIONISTS - BOOK 1

K. YORK

Kelley A. York
alleviating@gmail.com
www.kelley-york.com

Cover design by Sleepy Fox Studio – www.sleepyfoxstudio.net
Interior design by Sleepy Fox Studio – www.sleepyfoxstudio.net
Editing by Karen Meeus Editing – www.karenmeeusediting.com

E-book ASIN/ISBN 978-1-960322-08-1
Paperback ISBN 978-1-960322-09-8
First Edition June 1, 2023

GLASS CASTLES

by

K. YORK

CONTENT WARNING:

The following story contains references to real historical happenings, including bodysnatching (digging up graves), period-appriorate homophobia, innacurate beliefs regarding epilepsy, and more. All sexual scenes involved are consensual and there is no sexual abuse of any kind.

LONDON, 1870s

ONE

Lucas's stomach let out a deep, rumbling growl, the sort one only heard from a belly that hadn't seen any decent food in days, and yet the sound was drowned out by the merrymaking of patrons all about the pub, men talking and laughing and drinking and, yes, eating. Lucas watched for any plates to be left behind that might contain a couple of scraps he could sneak into his mouth before the aproners cleared them away.

To say that he was embarrassed to be reduced to such a thing was an understatement. If he could bring himself to abandon his pride once in a while, it would make survival a hell of a lot easier.

He'd put all sorts of thought into what he could do to get some coin in his pockets. Thievery had crossed his mind, but Lucas was nothing if not honest, and the thought of someone else going without because of him didn't sit right in his gut. Factory work wasn't an option—likely never would be again, damn it all—and he was no longer of a small enough build to fit down chimneys or to go crawling around in sewers to catch rats.

A figure slid into the chair across from him, and Lucas cast him a brief look. "I was beginning to think you'd taken the night off."

Jasper gave him a smile that reached his dark eyes. It was no surprise that all the men at The Rusty Duck liked him with a smile like that, Lucas thought, and also no surprise they often paid to get him alone into a back room. It was not a life his friend enjoyed, but it kept him fed, kept a roof over his head, and it was the only life Jasper had known since he was a child.

Admittedly, Lucas had put some of his own consideration into following in Jasper's footsteps. He was hungry enough to try almost anything.

"I never take a Friday off. I thought you might share some dinner with me," Jasper said, elbows propped upon the table and his chin nestled into his palm. "You look like you could use a bite to eat."

It was carefully masked charity, but charity, nonetheless. Lucas almost took him up on it. Almost. "I ate this mornin'," he lied, overturning an empty glass between them on the table. It had contained a smidge of gin when he'd sat down after the last patron left, and he'd finished it off, grateful for *something* in his belly.

"Liar."

"I ain't lyin'."

"You've been sitting here for thirty minutes, eyeing the other tables like you might slaughter them just for a scrap of their food."

Lucas huffed but did not argue that bit of truth.

Jasper reached across the table and touched his arm. "I promise, I can afford it, if you're hungry."

"I'm not lookin' for handouts, Jasper."

"You would do the same for me if our situations were reversed. I'm pretty sure you *have*, in fact, when I've been short on funds."

"Yeah, well…" He trailed off, gaze traversing across the faces in the tavern. Faces that were mostly familiar to him, in some shape or form. These were men who'd been sneaking away from their families and wives for years. Some of them came for a quick shag in the rooms upstairs. Most of them, though, simply showed up to have a drink in the company of men like them. Men with *skewed preferences*, most outsiders would say. Lucas was no different, and he'd spent his fair share of nights sneaking away upstairs to a rented room with the promise of having another man's mouth on his cock.

He bit briefly at his lower lip, surveying the patrons with thought. He'd fucked men for years for fun, so would doing it to turn a profit really be so different? He'd spoken to Jasper about it at length, about how he did it, how he had stomached some of the men who bedded him… Jasper had shrugged it off. *You do what you have to do. You try to see the beauty in people, even when it isn't immediately apparent. Or you pretend you're somewhere else.*

A depressing thought, that. To simply close one's eyes and bear through it. But maybe Jasper was right: people did what they had to do in order to survive.

In his search for a face he was certain he did not know, Lucas's gaze came to rest upon a man seated far off in the corner, alone, nursing a mug of ale and a mostly untouched bowl of meat and vegetables. He looked, for all intents and purposes, like he didn't belong there amongst the riff-raff. Clean, well-dressed, put-together. A proper gentleman, really. Clearly a man who did not spend his days toiling away at a machine or in the mines or begging for money on the street.

There's got to be far nicer pubs than this one for men like us, Lucas thought, but what would he know about the life of the well-heeled?

He wet his lips. This could be some sort of sign, couldn't it? Well-dressed gent, clearly had some money to him, looked too uncomfortable about being there to approach anyone himself, so maybe—

Maybe.

Jasper touched his arm at some point, informing him he needed to go, and Lucas gave him a brief nod while keeping his gaze on the gentleman. The fact that all that food was largely going to waste was making his stomach growl in disdain. But, when the man finally retrieved his hat and cane and rose to his feet, leaving the food and drink behind, Lucas made the split-second decision to follow him out of the pub instead of swooping in on the remains.

It would figure that it had started to rain, just a light sprinkling with the threat of something worse as the night progressed. Lucas yanked his cap snugly onto his head with a grimace and a shiver, catching sight of the gentleman slipping down the alley, away from the obscure entrance to the pub, and towards the street.

This entire idea is fuckin' mad. Lucas shook off the uneasiness building in his chest and trotted after the stranger. Better to try this away from the crowds; rejection would be a bigger blow to his ego with an audience present. This man with the nice hat and nice coat strolling down the street was likely to laugh in his face, but—it was worth a go. To practise, if nothing else.

They walked a few roads over, taking the occasional turn, with Lucas keeping a careful distance and waiting for the opportune moment to approach, all while trying to think of what to say. Then the man ducked down another alley, and Lucas paused for half a second, swore under his breath, and jogged to catch up.

He rounded the entrance to the alley and damn near collided with the stranger.

Up close, the man's wealth and good breeding were even more apparent. He smelled of orange spices and soaps, his face clean-shaven, and his chestnut-brown hair recently trimmed, the gentle waves tamed ever so carefully and swept back from his face. Everything from his coat to his tie was immaculately cared for and tailored to fit...

And he stared at Lucas with a most unimpressed glower on his handsome face.

"So, what is it then?" he asked in a clipped tone.

Lucas took an abrupt step back, the words catching in his throat. "I— sorry?"

"Planning to pickpocket me, or will you rob me at knifepoint instead?" The man didn't grant him much space. He closed the distance Lucas had tried to put between them, and the several inches he had on Lucas made him feel incredibly small.

Lucas opened his mouth to a startled 'O', realisation setting in. "N-no,

GLASS CASTLES

neither?"

The man pursed his lips, brows knitting together. "Neither."

"I ain't a thief!"

"Aren't you? You certainly look like one. If you weren't planning to rob me, why were you following me?"

"I saw you at The Rusty Duck, and I was plannin' on making you an offer, is all!"

The other man paused. His hands, which were folded atop the head of his cane, tightened enough that the fabric of his gloves creaked. "Planning on blackmailing me, then."

Lucas scoffed. "You're shit at this guessing game. I was there, too. You think I wanna get the place shut down by goin' to the bobbies? I had a...a proposition. Of sorts. Regardin' me and you." Christ, why was this so difficult? He'd seen Jasper do this sort of thing for years with ease and an elegance Lucas could not even pretend he possessed.

"A proposition..." The frown vanished from the gentleman's face. The corners of his mouth ticked up into something far too close to amusement for Lucas's liking. "*You're* a whore?"

Heat pricked his cheeks. What the hell did *that* mean? Sure, his clothes were a bit of a tattered mess, and he was in dire need of a haircut and a bath, but so it was with most every other man in that tavern. He knew damned well he wasn't a terrible-looking lad—enough good-looking men had told him so. He cleaned up nice too, when the occasion presented itself. "I'm... I'm not exactly..."

The gentleman smirked. "I may be shit at guessing games, but you're shit at propositioning men on the street."

Lucas contemplated the merits of simply turning and making a run for it. But he'd made the decision to do this, and he'd come all this way, foregoing this man's leftovers on the slim chance he might earn enough money for a couple of proper meals. "Yeah, well, I know enough to know gents like you

- 13 -

don't often come to our neighbourhood unless they got no other choice. Likely someone who don't wanna risk being spotted at a pub like that in his own neck of the woods, yeah? So you come to 'slum it', maybe find company for the night, but you chickened out and left alone. Trust me, you ain't the first fancy bloke who's done it."

The gentleman gave him a long and thoughtful stare and then tapped his cane once against the cobblestone. "*Well*, you have everything figured out, don't you?"

The way he said it made Lucas feel he didn't have a damned thing figured out at all. His shoulders hunched, but he raised his chin high as though proper posture might make up for the head of height difference between them.

When Lucas didn't answer—in large part because he couldn't think what to say—the gentleman tipped the brim of his top hat and smiled.

"It was interesting to meet you, but I'm afraid I'll be declining your... generous offer, and I must be going." Then, as he turned to leave, he stopped again. The hesitation made Lucas's insides flip about nervously, wondering if the man was having second thoughts. He turned back to Lucas and gave him a more thorough once-over. "However, if it's work that you're after, I might have something available."

From his pocket, he produced a trade card, which Lucas took out of reflex. The stiff paper was simplistic in design. A blue-inked border, an address, and a name.

Henry Glass
Surgeon

By the time Lucas had read it over and looked up again, the gentleman— Mr Glass—had already begun to walk away down the alley, leaving Lucas alone in the dark.

Who does he think he is? he thought sourly as he slumped against the nearby wall. *I don't need no handouts. Also don't need to work for no stuck-up rich bloke, neither.*

And yet, as he looked down at the trade card, he couldn't bring himself simply to discard it. Instead, he tucked it into a back pocket and made his way back out onto the street. Maybe he'd return to The Rusty Duck and take Jasper up on that offer of a meal, just this once.

TWO

Not for the first time, Lucas slept in the alley outside The Rusty Duck. Once in a while, he would sleep at Jasper's place, but only when Madam Beatrice wasn't likely to catch him. She was a fussy old bat, a madam who ran a less than tidy brothel, and the rooms the whores occupied were hardly large enough to fit a bed and a tiny dresser.

In Lucas's encounters with her over the years, she'd seen him as nothing more than a lowlife looking for a free fuck—which he wasn't—and a free place to lay his head—which, well, all right, he was. But he was firmly of the opinion that since Jasper paid his way at the establishment, it ought to be his choice what to do with his space.

Still, Lucas suspected Jasper got a good tongue-lashing any time they were caught, so he saved those nights for only the direst of situations. Such as when the weather took a particularly nasty turn or, like last winter, when he came down with a miserable sickness and Jasper had to feign illness himself to lock them both away in his cold, draughty room while Lucas recovered.

So, the alley it was. When he woke, it was to the sound of snoring from nearby. Likely some bloke who'd staggered out of the tavern in the early hours of the morning, too drunk to make it home. Lucas, meanwhile, had given in and wolfed down a small but appreciated meal from Jasper, chased it with a single dram of gin, and called it a night.

He had important things to do today that would not be done well with a bottle ache, after all.

In the early morning hours, Lucas nibbled on some of the jerky he had left over from his supper the previous night. Afterwards, he headed to The Sun and Stars, the bawdyhouse Jasper worked at, which was only a few blocks away. He climbed to the rooftop of the neighbouring building and scooted to the edge where he was able to reach across the ridiculously small distance between the cramped buildings to rap upon Jasper's window.

It took a moment, but the ratty curtains were pushed aside, and Jasper's face peered out at him, bleary-eyed and sleep deprived. The window opened not a second later, and despite the early hour and the fact Jasper had likely worked late into the night, he did nothing less than greet Lucas with a warm smile.

"Cleaning up then?" he asked, stepping back as Lucas unceremoniously clambered his way from the roof through the window.

"Inquirin' about another job today, down at Fischer's canning place." He flashed his friend a hopeful grin, wasting no time in beginning to undress.

Jasper crouched to open the bottom drawer of his dresser, where he'd stashed Lucas's meagre few belongings for him, and retrieved the only somewhat decent outfit Lucas owned. "Another factory? Lu…"

"Don't do that. Could be different this time, y'never know." Lucas discarded his clothes, stepped around Jasper to the washbasin atop the dresser, and set to scrubbing himself down as much as he was able with the freezing cold water from the pitcher. No real substitute for a proper bath, but God knew when he last had one of those; if he didn't have the money to eat, he certainly didn't have the money to visit a bathhouse.

Jasper had a seat on the edge of the bed, clothes folded in his lap. "Just promise you won't be terribly upset if they turn you down."

"I won't be terribly upset," Lucas said, turning with the flat razor in hand and pointing it at him, " 'cause they ain't gonna turn me down. I'm a damned good worker. You know I am!"

"You *are*."

"And someone's gonna see that and give me a job." With an indignant sniff that suggested the conversation was over, he turned back to the mirror. He had a limited amount of time to wash and shave and dress, and then sneak back out the way he came before Madam Beatrice did her rounds to ensure everyone was accounted for—and alone.

He took his leave after finishing off the last of the jerky from the night before, jogging down the street towards the docks a few miles away.

This part of town still left a bad taste in Lucas's mouth. Nothing there reminded him of good things. Fischer's Canning Factory wasn't one of the better-paying joints in the area, nor were the working conditions fantastic… and that was saying something. But it went back to that whole *swallowing his pride* thing. Lucas knew when he'd been beaten. He knew he was running out of options.

Which was why he'd presented himself to Mr Fischer's assistants a week prior, touting his experience, careful to leave out certain past incidents, and he'd been stunned when they had agreed to arrange a meeting.

Now, he presented himself again at the factory and was brought to the back where Mr Fischer's office sat. He stood before Fischer's desk, cap in hand, wringing it tightly between his fingers as he rambled off his qualifications yet again, this time to Mr Fischer himself.

Mr Fischer didn't even offer him a seat, although he hadn't bothered to get up from his own chair, either. He nudged his spectacles up the bridge of his hawkish nose, eyes on the papers upon his desk. "The hours are seven to five, Monday through Saturday, with overtime as needed. Payment is thirteen shillings a week. Does that sound satisfactory to you?"

Lucas bit back the questions on the tip of his tongue. Any other factory in the area could have had that wage beat by a couple of shillings, easy. "Yes, sir."

Mr Fischer smiled, but it was the sort of smile that didn't reach beyond his mouth. He looked like a man who'd never seen a day of hard labour in his life. Likely, he was from a moderately well-to-do family, perhaps with a relative or two who invested in this business. It was too new to have been handed down. But men like Mr Fischer didn't get to where they were by being nice or kind, especially not to their workers.

"You mentioned having been employed at Whitaker's a year ago, is that right?"

"Yeah, that's right, sir."

"Any particular reason why you left? I've heard he's still short on workers."

He twisted the cap in his hands, heartbeat picking up. He'd practised the answer to this a hundred times, but he was a shit liar. "We had a disagreement on wages, sir. Which I'm sure won't be an issue here. I've heard nothin' but good things from your staff." It came out more convincing than he expected, thank God, but the words felt all wrong on his tongue.

"Is that right?" Mr Fischer finally lifted his head and reclined in his seat, steepling his fingers before himself. "Sometimes a job isn't a good fit for everyone."

Lucas swallowed hard past a dry throat and maintained a nervous smile. "If you'd be willing to give me a chance, you'll see how hard a worker I am."

"I suspect that I would. Except, Mr Walker…" Mr Fischer raised his eyebrows. "I'm curious to hear more about this previous job at Whitaker's. You see, I've heard from your previous employer that your 'disagreement' regarding your wages was a bit more than a mere dispute."

Dread washed over him like a cold wave, settling bone deep. "Sir?"

"Businessmen talk, Mr Walker. I'm afraid there's no room for upstarts in this industry, and certainly not in my factory."

"I—I don't understand. If you knew, why'd you agree to see me in the first place?"

"*I* did not agree to anything. My assistants did. Now, I believe Mr Tap at Whitaker's told you when you were let go that you'd be hard-pressed to land another position in the East End. He was not lying."

The dread was swiftly overtaken by panic. *No, no, no...* "Sir, *please*. I swear to you, it's different now. Just give me a chance—"

Mr Fischer adjusted his glasses and gave a dismissive wave of his hand. "Good day, Mr Walker."

He thought to throw himself to the floor, to cast himself at the man's mercy and beg. But apparently his pride hadn't been stamped out entirely, because the disappointment and anger rose like bile in his throat, making it difficult to formulate any coherent, rational response.

This was his last hope for employment, and he'd lost it.

Fuck.

A clerk showed him back out into the cold. At least for a little while, he'd been able to enjoy the warmth of the factory, the sort of sweltering heat that felt nice for a bit, but Lucas knew would become overwhelming after long hours of work there.

He took up a seat near the docks, overlooking the water, idly watching crews load and unload their ships—also not an option for him, he'd already attempted it and found he got unbearably seasick—and tried not to pay any mind to the scent of cooked fish and dried meats from nearby vendor carts. He was starving, disheartened, and frustrated. Not to mention, he had no interest in returning to the brothel just yet and having to face the pitying looks from his best mate.

How *stupid* he'd been to be so confident and have such high hopes. Jasper had tried to tell him as much, hadn't he? And now Lucas would be crawling back to admit Jasper was right, that he'd made a mess of his entire life, and the options presented to him now...

He was likely to remain homeless and unemployed. No factory here would take him, he clearly wasn't cut out to be a rent boy, and no office or store was likely to hire a man like him. Being able-bodied meant even the workhouses would turn him away because he wasn't in need enough.

Might still be one option left.

He reached into his cap where he'd tucked the trade card from the previous night.

Henry Glass.

What sort of work would a surgeon possibly have for the likes of him? He was hardly educated, didn't know a damned thing about...surgeoning...stuff. Though he supposed a surgeon in clothes that nice and in a place like the West End would have the money to pay someone handsomely for whatever-it-was.

Lucas bit the inside of his cheek and tugged his cap back on, still studying the card. The listed address was clear across town, and it was getting to be afternoon. If this address was for a place of business and not a residence, he ought to have just enough time to get there and find this Mr Glass.

As he pushed to his feet and began the trek, he tried not to get his spirits too high. But when his hopes were already swimming at rock bottom, there was little place for them to go but up.

THREE

The hospitals were miserable places. Lucas avoided them at all costs. He'd watched his father die in one and, although he'd been too young to remember, his mother had died in one too. While he was sure the physicians and surgeons did their best, there was little to be done for overcrowding, poor funding, and the sheer number of people seeking treatment. Of course, the poor would have more health issues—crowded dwellings, overflowing outhouses shared between three and four families, unclean drinking water… Not to mention the lack of fresh air thanks to the local factories.

For half an hour, Lucas lingered outside, hoping to catch sight of Mr Glass coming or going from the hospital so that he needn't step inside. When he grew too impatient—and too worried he might miss him altogether—he gritted his teeth, adjusted his cap, and entered the building.

Even the waiting hall was packed, mothers with wailing, coughing children, men with various appendages in slings and braces, one woman coughing wetly into her handkerchief… Lucas shrunk in on himself, inching down the narrow aisle of benches to a desk where a haggard, tired woman was explaining to a husband of a pregnant wife that he'd need to take a seat, just like the rest of them.

"She's been havin' contractions since last night; she's like to give birth right here on the damn floor!" the man snapped in a rough, Irish brogue.

The woman gave a tired sigh. "She wouldn't be the first. Promise, soon as I can get a bed free, she'll go back. I'll send for someone in the meantime."

The man glowered, but his tired wife coaxed him away from the desk to take a seat nearby. Lucas watched them go, pityingly, until he noticed the nurse watching him.

"Well? What's it, then?" She looked him over, likely noting the lack of visible injury or illness.

"Right, um—Is Mr... that is, Doctor Glass, in? I was asked to call on him," Lucas stammered. When the woman only stared at him dispassionately, he produced the trade card. It had got a bit wrinkled from him clutching it so tight most of the trip there. Still, she took a look at it, arched an eyebrow, and pointed down the hall.

"He's in surgery right now and not to be disturbed. You can wait for him across from the operating theatre, if you must."

Lucas forced himself to relax. He opened his mouth to thank her, but she had already turned her attention to the next group of people demanding to be heard, and Lucas quickly cleared the area.

The hallway was significantly quieter. At least, it was void of patients. Chairs and windows lined the leftmost wall, every window opened wide to allow in as much fresh air as possible. Nothing was worse than a stuffy hospital with a bunch of sick people. Nurses and physicians alike hurried back and forth, never a lull, never a leisurely moment.

Given that there were several doors leading to operating rooms, Lucas had a seat where he could keep an eye on all of them should the good doctor emerge. He held his cap in his hands, mulling over just what he ought to say when he saw the man again. *Evenin', I know I propositioned you the other night— offer's still open, by the by—but thought I'd see if you'd give me some work.*

Christ, he was no good at this.

He hunched forward in his seat, pushing a hand through his hair. Maybe this trip was a mistake. Maybe he ought to have returned to Jasper, metaphorical tail between his legs, begged another meal off him, and asked Madam Beatrice if she had a spare room he might take on while he had Jasper show him the ropes of being a good and proper rent boy. Humiliating as it might be, it was preferable to starving or being forced to leave the only home he'd ever known.

There was no way to tell how much time ticked by, but it certainly felt like a good two hours, if not longer. The sun had begun to dip outside, and Lucas inwardly grimaced at the idea of walking home in the dark. He was likely better off finding a place to hide out near the hospital and hope some constable didn't come barking at him to move along.

Finally, after a small eternity, the doors to the auditorium directly across from Lucas swung open. A group of men in tidy suits emerged, notebooks in hand, chatting amongst themselves. For a moment, Lucas worried when he didn't see Mr Glass among them.

Glass ended up being one of the last to exit the room, looking startlingly different without his top hat or cane, now donning an apron stained with red. It looked terribly fresh, too, a thought which made Lucas's stomach roll. He pushed to his feet swiftly, cap clutched tight, and waited to be noticed. Except Glass didn't see him at all, too focused on the men around him, eager students drinking up every ounce of information he was willing to bestow.

Before he could get too far down the hall, Lucas found his voice again. "'Scuse me? Mr Glass?"

This time, Henry Glass stopped and turned to look. Recognition dawned on his handsome face, his eyebrows arching. Lucas had halfway expected him simply to continue along, ignoring him completely, but—

"Pardon me, gentlemen." He gestured for the students to be on their way. Once the hall had mostly cleared, the surgeon approached him with a mildly inquisitive twist to his mouth. "We meet again. I'll admit, I didn't think I'd be seeing you. Or are you only here because you've fallen ill…?"

"I ain't sick," Lucas said, face warming. He thrust out his hand, offering the card to Glass, which was a ridiculous gesture, he realised, given that Glass was the one who gave him the damned thing and what would he do with a crumpled, damp trade card now? "You said somethin' about work. So, here I am."

Glass's eyes dropped to the card, thoughtful, though he didn't take it. "Indeed. Come with me." He turned on his heel and started off down the hall, and Lucas scurried after him, having to widen his stride to keep up with the taller man.

Lucas couldn't help but survey the state of Mr Glass. The scent of rubbing alcohol and blood clung to him. Had Glass been in there that whole time operating on a patient? Explaining aloud his procedure to knowledge-hungry students and the casual onlooker? He wanted to ask but wasn't certain how to word it without sounding like a fool.

Glass took a door nearby, one that opened to another—empty—auditorium. They headed down the steep steps and through another door across the observatory that led into a back room. In there, Lucas saw rows of cubbies and hooks adorned with aprons, hats, coats, bags, and other personal belongings of the physicians and surgeons who worked there. Glass himself stripped out of the smock he was wearing, hanging it next to a row of other soiled garments. The sight of them reminded Lucas more of a butcher's shop than a hospital.

"Something the matter?" Glass asked.

Lucas whipped around towards the sound of his voice. "What? No."

Glass began to roll down his sleeves where they'd been previously pushed up to his elbows. "Something on your mind, then?"

Lucas faltered. "Were you...cuttin' someone up in that room?"

The surgeon cracked a smile. "I was saving a man's life, but yes, that did involve a bit of 'cutting up'."

"He's all right, then?"

"Barring any infection, he will make a full recovery."

"Good. S'good." Lucas placed the cap back upon his head and crammed his hands into his pockets. "So…the work you want me to do, it ain't gonna involve cuttin' people, right?"

As he stepped to a mirror on the wall to adjust his cufflinks and then his tie, Glass laughed. "Goodness, no. No cutting involved. However, I'm a bit reluctant to go offering you employment doing much of anything just yet."

Lucas squared his shoulders. "What? Why? You asked me here!"

"I did. Though typically when one is looking for employment, one should at least have the common sense to introduce oneself first."

Lucas paused, mouth agape. No, he never had given his name, had he? He thrust out a hand. "Lucas Walker. S'nice to meet you. Er, properly."

There was a delightful little crinkle to the surgeon's eyes when he smiled. He extended a hand to give Lucas's a shake. It was, Lucas noted, thankfully clean. Likely cleaner than his own, if he was honest.

"Henry Glass. Pleasure to meet you, Mr Walker."

"Just Lucas. Please." The sound of *Mr Walker* on a gentleman's tongue made him feel wrong, unworthy. Patronised. The only times he'd ever heard it spoken in such a way were by men addressing his father or said condescendingly by blokes like Mr Fischer. Men higher above him in position and money and every other status in the world.

Mr Glass withdrew his hand and beckoned to a nearby table and chairs, the former which was stacked with medical texts and a few loose papers. Lucas sat a little more abruptly than was necessary, but his body was alight with nervousness, making him fidgety and wanting to crawl out of his own skin.

Glass said, "Might I ask what sort of work you're looking for?"

"Anythin'," Lucas admitted. "Been a bit down on my luck. Willin' to take on whatever puts some food on the table."

Glass sat across from him, an arm resting on the table, one leg crossed neatly over the other. "Anything? Even whoring, it seems."

It didn't sound so much like an accusation as it did an observation, but it rankled Lucas all the same. He slouched forward with his hands clasped atop the table, though maintaining eye contact when he was feeling vulnerable and embarrassed was damned near impossible. "If I got to, yeah."

"Why is it you haven't sought employment with one of the factories?"

"If it's all the same to you, Mr Glass, I don't really see how it matters."

"Doesn't it?"

He wrung his hands together so tightly that his knuckles mottled white. "I'm a damned good worker, sir. I think that's the important thing."

"Not afraid of physical labour?"

"Not a bit."

Glass tipped his head. "Glad to hear it. May I see that card I gave you?"

Lucas unfurled his hands and again retrieved the card from his pocket to offer it out. Glass took it, smoothed it out on the table, and plucked a pen from the stack of papers and books to write something across the blank side. He slid it back over to Lucas, who surveyed the neat script with a frown.

"What's this?"

"My address. If you'll join me for supper tomorrow evening, we can discuss your potential employment."

He stilled, fingertips just shy of the card as his gaze flicked up to the other man. "You want me over for supper? Why can't we talk about it now?"

"Because," Glass said, rising from his seat, "it's of a sensitive nature, and I have patients who require my attention. Tomorrow. Six o'clock. Am I to assume you'll be there?"

Supper. At some undoubtedly lovely house in a lovely neighbourhood with this lovely and proper well-to-do gent? Lucas could think of a thousand other things he'd rather do, a thousand other things that would involve much less humiliation on his part.

And yet, just like the night before, Glass seemed to take his silence as agreement because he smiled and escorted him out of the hospital, and Lucas never did manage to give him a straight answer.

FOUR

Henry Glass had many regrets in life.

Though to be perfectly fair, he knew very few people who didn't.

His regret was what had brought him to The Rusty Duck a few evenings ago. For many reasons, it was hardly the type of establishment he allowed himself to frequent, but now and again even he felt loneliness creeping in amid his self-imposed solitude and it shoved him out of his realm of comfort, seeking…something, anything, to fill that void.

Being there brought about an immediate sense of anxiety even though, being a fair distance from home, he was not likely to run into anyone he knew and, even if he had, they would have been there for reasons similar to his own. It wasn't even that Henry was nervous about what trouble it could spell out for him and his career, but more so that he had no interest in knowing that people were out there harbouring his secrets. There were enough of them already.

As he'd scanned the room, though, he'd forced himself to relax. Not one familiar face after all. Perhaps he could enjoy his evening in peace. Perhaps he would even strike up a conversation with someone… After he finished his drink to bolster his courage, of course.

Except as he reached the bottom of that drink, he had found himself ordering another. Looking for excuses to sit there alone, no doubt, but everyone seemed to be already engaged or gave the impression they had no interest in conversation.

He had gazed upon the room as though hoping to meet someone's eye and feel some sort of *spark*. Once upon a time, he'd met a man in a bookstore, someone with whom he'd held an immediate connection. That man had long since left Henry's life—left a gaping, raw wound in his heart that never had quite healed—and he supposed it was foolishness on his part to expect some sort of instantaneous, soul-defining connection with anyone like that ever again.

With his third drink, Henry had ordered some food as well. Better than sitting there like some sad drunk alone in a public house, drinking away his sorrows. At least eating gave him some illusion of normalcy. Never mind that the food somehow managed to taste even less appetising than the sad excuse for alcohol they had served him.

But what had begun as one drink and turned into several and a largely untouched bowl of food resulted in Henry leaving without saying anything to anyone beyond a few orders to the barkeep and a murmured apology for bumping into someone on his way out. Not so much as a *hello* to a single stranger, and he'd felt so bloody drained and disappointed with himself.

Almost immediately he had noticed he was being followed by some tired-looking youth who couldn't have been older than his early twenties, and then he was being propositioned in the middle of a dark alley.

Though he'd be a liar if he didn't later admit to himself that, for a brief moment, he'd considered it. Not the idea of paying just anyone for their company, no, but spending an evening with this young man in particular. Despite the lad's tattered, dirty appearance, with those bright blue eyes peering at him from beneath a mop of blond hair and sun-darkened skin, there was just *something* about him that had struck Henry soundly in the chest.

Offering out his card had been just as ridiculous as Mr Walker's offer, when he reflected on it later. For whatever kindness he tried to extend out to others—particularly those of his persuasion—Henry didn't give work to just anyone he met on the street. Daniel handled that aspect, and Henry trusted his judgement. More than his own, really. Daniel brought him people he thought worthy; Henry paid them for their labour. Simple as that.

Perhaps the offer of work had been an excuse, though. Perhaps he could say he didn't know what possessed him, that he felt exceptionally sympathetic towards this wide-eyed man in barely more than rags, but at the end of the day…

If he forced himself to be honest, Henry would have to reluctantly admit he was simply searching for a reason to see him again.

And then there the young man was, standing in the hospital hallway, looking so charmingly out of place while Henry and a gaggle of students all turned to stare at him. Just like that, Henry's attention had shifted.

It remained shifted, long after Lucas Walker had left. Henry found himself more than once pausing to glance at his pocket watch, noting that the afternoon had been dragging. In reality, he could have had a conversation with Mr Walker just fine in the comfort of his office; he wasn't *truly* concerned about the privacy they did or did not have. It was a hapless attempt to have Mr Walker's undivided attention in a more private space, although Henry wouldn't have a clue what to do with it once he had it.

After work, he hurried home and informed Frederick that they'd be having company the following evening and to see to it that supper would be prepared. Frederick had handled this sudden change of plans with the grace that he did most things.

"Will it be some of your colleagues joining us, sir?"

Henry put up his greatcoat and hat, offering a small smile to his longtime butler. "No, not this time. Just…someone I met when I went out the other evening."

Perhaps his smile gave too much away, however; Frederick had known him for the better part of a decade now, and the look he gave his employer was most curious. "Someone you met, sir?"

With a bit of a cough, Henry moved farther into the hall, intending to head to his study until dinner. "That's what I said."

"Very good. I'll see to it we prepare something extra nice for your just-someone-you-met." Henry could hear the quiet amusement in his voice.

An instantaneous connection? He wasn't sure about that. But perhaps his venture to The Rusty Duck had not been entirely in vain after all.

FIVE

"This is the only decent outfit I got," Lucas lamented the following afternoon, "and he's already seen me in it."

Jasper sat with his legs folded on his bed, elbows upon his knees, watching Lucas as he observed himself in the mirror. "Hm. Well, I've got a few dresses, if you'd rather."

"You're fuckin' hilarious."

"Oh, all right. What about a different necktie? Just to change it up a bit."

Lucas tugged at the frayed hem of his shirt. He didn't even own a proper collar, nor cufflinks, nor even a tie or cravat. Aside from his weatherworn cap, he had no hat to call his own, and his boots were hardly proper shoes for supper at anyone's house, let alone a gentleman's. "Or I could spare myself and not go."

His friend sighed and slipped from the bed to step up behind him. Jasper was waifish and delicate in every way a man possibly could be, and yet he still stood taller than Lucas by a few inches. From a dresser drawer, he retrieved a necktie and held it to Lucas's chest to get an idea of how it would look.

"You were willing to swallow your pride enough to proposition a man in a dark alley but not enough to have a meal with him?"

"That was different," Lucas muttered, almost wishing he hadn't told Jasper about the other night. "I'd never have had to see him again."

A thin smile pulled at Jasper's mouth. "If you did a proper job, you would have. They always come back if it's good."

"I'll keep that in mind, I guess."

Jasper turned him around, draping the fabric about his neck and setting to tying it with practised ease. He could do it with his eyes closed, and it'd likely look better than anything Lucas could manage. Not for the first time, Lucas marvelled at how someone from Jasper's background could be so…refined. Elegant. Articulate. He spoke and moved and acted like someone well above his class. "Whoever this Mr Glass is, he's obviously seen something in you he likes. He's a good judge of character."

"Or he's plannin' on carvin' me up in one of them operating theatres."

"Don't be silly. Although there are days I could stand for a surgeon to sew your mouth shut." He smoothed the tie and the front of Lucas's rumpled shirt, then brought his hands to his friend's shoulders. "There. You look handsome."

Lucas frowned. "I look like a frog pretending to be a prince."

"Smile. It makes all the difference."

"*Tch.*"

"I mean it." He stepped back, hands on his hips. "You can fuss and gripe about it on your way there. I have work to get to, and you—well, if nothing else, you'll get a good meal out of the evening, hm?"

During his trip across the city—Jasper insisted on giving him enough money to catch a hansom cab there—Lucas tried to keep those last words in mind. He had already made a fool of himself in front of this man. Could it really get much worse?

As expected, Henry Glass lived in a beautiful terrace home in a respectable neighbourhood. Lucas disembarked from the cab and peered up at the three-storey building before him. His insides promptly tangled themselves into knots. There was nothing about this evening that was likely to have him feeling anything other than insignificant and small.

But the cab was already pulling away, horse hooves clopping merrily along the street, so unless he wanted to walk home, he had no choice but to ascend the front steps and knock.

An older man in dark-blue livery answered the door. He gave a toothy smile and stepped back, allowing Lucas inside. Beneath his other arm, he held a small, wriggling terrier, who looked very eager to get loose so it might excitedly throw itself at Lucas. It reminded Lucas of the dogs he worked with as a child, hunting rats in the sewers.

"Good evening, Mr Walker. May I take your coat?"

His coat? Oh. Lucas looked down at himself. He didn't own an overcoat, and his shirt had seen better days; he'd thought that it wouldn't be of much concern because his jacket would hide it. *So much for that.* Inwardly grimacing, he slid from his coat and offered it to the butler, who proceeded to hang it for him and then led him down the hall.

Lucas tried to think if he'd ever had cause to step into such a lovely house before and came up empty. Everything, from the detailed moulding and the intricate wallpaper to the wainscoting and the tiled floors, shined to perfection and was like something from a dream. Every step he took, Lucas felt like he was dirtying the space by occupying it.

It was a sensation that did not alleviate any when the butler brought him into the dining hall. The table was large enough to seat fifteen people, if not more, and despite it being only him and Mr Glass in the room, the entire length of the table had been decorated as though prepared for an entire dinner party. A server had already begun to bring out dishes, and Lucas wondered if he was a little late after all.

Mr Glass, seated at the head of the table, rose smoothly and greeted Lucas with a warm smile.

"Mr Walker. So glad you could join me tonight."

He was dressed more like he'd been that night at The Rusty Duck, Lucas noted. Crisp, clean clothes and not a hair out of place. He looked dashingly handsome, for that matter, and it reminded Lucas of why he originally even thought to follow him out of the tavern.

"Am I late?" Lucas asked, lingering there at the opposite end of the table, unsure what proper etiquette dictated he ought to do. Glass gestured to an empty seat to his right, where another place had been set, so Lucas forced his legs to cooperate and moved further into the room.

Glass didn't quite answer his question but gave a dismissive wave to imply it didn't matter. "I hope you're hungry."

"Famished, actually." Lucas could not stop his eyes from constantly flicking to the serving trays. Meats, potatoes, soups, breads. More food in one place than he'd ever seen. That it was food available for him to eat made it even more enticing. His stomach gave a plaintive growl that Lucas hoped was obscured somewhat by the scratching of the chair legs as he scooted it in close.

"Good. Go on. Help yourself."

Lucas paused, nerves on edge. He knew damned well there was a method to this, manners he ought to be displaying, certain cutlery he should be using at specific times. So, he tried to watch Glass from the corner of his gaze, attempting to mimic him and eat what he ate, despite his overwhelming urge to cram as much food down his gullet as he could, like he might somehow store it away to make up for all the days he'd gone hungry.

They spoke little. Save for the clink of cutlery against plates and the sound of glasses being refilled, the room remained quiet. It might have made him more nervous, except the silence was almost appreciated. Lucas wasn't certain he could handle maintaining polite conversation while trying to ensure he didn't make a fool of himself over his lack of knowledge of proper table etiquette.

He ate until his stomach hurt and he eyed the remaining food upon the table, disappointed he couldn't somehow manage to eat it all and wondering just what would happen to the leftovers. Would they be thrown out? Fed to the dog? The thought of so much going to waste made him feel terribly nauseated. Or maybe that was the result of stuffing himself.

"I take it the meal was to your liking," Glass remarked once the server returned to begin clearing the table.

Lucas swiped at his mouth with a napkin and reached for his third—fourth?—glass of wine. His cheeks warmed. Ought he be concerned that he'd committed some sort of misstep eating as much as he had? "It was delicious. Thank you."

"You're quite welcome." Glass tipped his head. "If you've had your fill, let's retire for a drink and talk business."

Another drink? Lucas watched him push back his chair and couldn't help but swiftly down the remainder of his own wine before getting up—wobbling, just a bit, on unsteady legs—to follow him from the dining room. They retreated into a parlour across the hall, lined with books and large, stuffed, comfortable-looking chairs, and a bar cart of more wine. Lucas took the seat Glass directed him to, folding his hands in his lap and sitting stiffly while the older man stepped to the bar cart.

"Dare I ask if you have a preference in your alcohol?"

"Uh." He scanned the bottles. At The Rusty Duck, he drank whatever swill he could get his paws on. But he suspected what Glass had in those bottles was leagues above whatever The Rusty Duck served. "Surprise me?"

Glass chuckled and turned away. Lucas forced himself to slump back in his chair and relax, taking a better look around the room. Knick-knacks and trinkets galore lined the shelves amongst the books. Paintings and sketches covered almost every inch of free wall space, including a beautifully rendered portrait of a woman above the fireplace mantel. She couldn't be much older than Lucas himself, with honey-coloured hair and deep hazel eyes, and a knowing smile upon her pretty mouth. Lucas had to admit, although his leanings were significantly more towards men, that such a woman would be the exact type he'd go for when the mood to be with one struck him.

Glass stepped up beside his chair, offering out a drink, which Lucas took without really looking at him. Lucas nodded to the painting. "Who's that?"

"Cordelia." Glass took a seat across from him, legs crossed, swirling the amber liquid about his cup while his gaze slanted sideways to observe the portrait. "My wife."

Lucas stilled. "Your…"

"She died." He smiled slightly. "Close to fifteen years ago now."

"I'm sorry for your loss." Was that odd to say when so much time had passed? Fifteen years ago, Lucas had been just a small child, and this man had already been married. Not that it ought to have surprised him, really. He estimated Mr Glass to be his senior by a decade or more—it was the manner in which he presented himself, the faint lines around his eyes, and the sprinkling of grey at his temples. He was the epitome of a middle-aged gentleman in all the ways that made Lucas a little weak in the knees.

"We were not wed long," Glass said. "Barely a year before she fell ill."

Lucas slid his thumb along the rim of his glass and looked down into it. "And you never remarried."

He chuckled. "You know why that is."

"Do I?"

"You saw me at that public house," he said absently. But before Lucas could question him further, he added, "Now, about that job."

Lucas exhaled heavily and took a long pull from his drink. Something told him he was going to need it. And he'd been right about the quality of it—certainly something he'd never had before. "Yeah, all right. I'm listenin'."

"As you well know, I am a surgeon. Part of my profession involves helping people. The other part…well, it involves *learning* how to help people. This includes a significant amount of research."

"Research?"

"On animals, mostly. I dissect a large number of goats and pigs."

"Oh." A pause. "What's that got to do with me?"

Glass smiled. "There's simply no substitute for using actual human bodies, Mr Walker—"

"Lucas."

"—and while the Anatomy Act has resulted in bodies becoming much more easily accessible, it can be tricky for surgeons such as myself to procure them for individualised research. Hoops to jump through, endless paperwork... And still, a shortage at times. The larger hospitals and anatomy schools always get first pick."

Lucas frowned. This conversation was leading somewhere, but he'd yet to grasp just where or what it had to do with the likes of him. "Uh-huh."

Glass took a sip from his drink and set it aside, distracted as the terrier from earlier came bouncing into the room and jumped into his lap. He began to scratch behind its ears. "Also particularly challenging when I'm in need of a specific type of body. Are you familiar with the name John Hunter?"

"Um, nope. Is he some kinda doctor?"

"He was, yes. Long since passed now. John Hunter was the sort of surgeon any man in the profession worth his salt could only dream of being. Some say he was out of his mind, but I've read his works, seen the drawings of the research he performed. He and his elder brother did significant research on the stages of gestation in women, for instance."

Glass must have realised the lost look on Lucas's face meant he was struggling to keep up with the conversation, and he shook his head. "I digress. Sometimes, my research includes finding bodies that fit certain criteria. People who died of specific illnesses, fitting certain demographics. There is no time to go through the proper channels to obtain them. And that means I need someone who can locate those bodies and bring them to me."

Lucas floundered. "But that's...that's against the law, ain't it?" He had met the occasional resurrection man, the blokes who raided the cemeteries at night to deliver bodies to the various hospitals and anatomy schools. He'd also seen and heard of them getting caught. They may have been a dying breed since the Anatomy Act, but they were far from extinct.

"Certainly not any more illegal than sodomy." Glass smiled, and heat blossomed across Lucas's face and slid all the way down to settle in his belly. "It's the dissection of the human body that is frowned upon by many, Mr Walker, and the theft of any items that might be buried with that body. A corpse is merely a corpse and not a possession, and therefore cannot be owned and cannot be stolen…so the law dictates."

Lucas's tongue swiped across his upper lip. "You want me to dig up bodies for you. What makes you think I'd ever do somethin' like that?"

"Because," Henry Glass said slowly, purposefully, as though he needed to articulate each word so Lucas could understand it, "you were attempting to solicit your body in a dark alley to a man you'd never met, far from anyone who could have helped you had I reacted violently. You did not even wait a few days before coming to see me about prospective work, and I suspect your reluctance to return to the factories is because you've been blacklisted for some reason or another."

He leaned forward then, which caused the dog to abandon his lap to jump to the floor. "Furthermore, you arrived here in the same suit you wore yesterday and devoured your food like you'd not eaten in weeks. You are jobless, perhaps even homeless or staying with someone on the merit of their good will, and you are desperate. The going price for a body is more than what any factory could ever hope to pay you. And please don't mistake me—I have a team who performs what I ask already, so I don't *need* you. But I think *you* need *me*. I think you need *this*."

Lucas would be lying if he tried to say it didn't sound appealing. Very, very appealing. But living in the areas he did, it was impossible not to have stumbled across the dead. Even working the sewers as a boy, he'd encountered his fair share of corpses. Drunkards and the destitute, men and women who'd crawled down there to die in the dark. The memory made him shudder, and he closed his eyes, trying to shake it off.

"What would this involve?" he asked.

"I would inform you when I'm in need of a cadaver. You and the other three men I employ would go to the cemetery promptly to procure the body and deliver it here to me." He tipped his head. "Any questions in more detail than that would be directed to the man you'd be working under."

His stomach rolled, but there was one thing that could have easily swayed him in one direction or the other, and that was, "How much is this gonna pay, exactly?"

"If the body is fresh enough that I can use it? Ten pounds, divided amongst the four of you."

Lucas nearly dropped his drink.

Hell, even if he got less for being new and inexperienced, that was still more than the measly fifteen shillings a week he'd got at his old job at Whitaker's. Certainly, it was more than what Mr Fischer would have paid.

He could get his own place. He could eat. He could pay Jasper back for all the meals and all the nights he'd snuck him inside to give Lucas a dry place to sleep.

He was completely mad for even considering this. He could end up in jail, get fined, turn into some sort of social pariah if anyone he knew found out what he was doing. Disturbing the dead might not be *entirely* illegal, but it sure as hell wasn't viewed nicely by society at large.

And yet, the prospect of a roof over his head and a full belly was too much to pass up. He finished off his drink in one fell swoop and bit back a nervous laugh.

"Yeah. All right. I guess I could give it a go."

SIX

Henry had all but flown home after work that afternoon. There were hours before Lucas Walker would arrive, but the extra time to prepare himself was appreciated. He'd given his menu requests to the cook that morning, and supper was well underway by the time he stepped through the door.

He was able to devote his full attention to making himself look presentable. It meant bathing, scrubbing the scent of the hospital from his person, leaving every inch of him pink and fresh. It meant shaving and restyling his hair, ensuring not a strand was out of place. As always, his clothing was in flawless condition, although he changed ties and waistcoats and shoes half a dozen times, puttering about like some sort of anxious schoolboy.

What followed was not the most eventful evening in history, but far from the worst. Then again, what had he anticipated? What had he expected? (What would he have *allowed*, at that?)

At least dinner was a success; Lucas had been so engrossed in what lay before him upon the table that it granted Henry time to watch him quietly, appreciating the angle of his jaw, the blue of his eyes, how he'd clearly gone through great lengths to make himself look nice although there was only so much he could do, given his wardrobe.

And, when Lucas took his leave, Henry reflected on the conversation and wondered if Daniel would be displeased with him.

Henry's small crew of resurrectionists had been working under him for shy of two years now, procuring bodies for his research. Aside from the initial hiring of one Daniel Barker, Henry had left the rest of the hiring to Daniel himself. Henry's only stipulations were that employees be men like them—with secrets to hide regarding their attraction towards other men—and that they truly *needed* the work.

He sent a letter the next morning with the first post of the day, requesting Daniel's company when he had a moment. Nothing of dire importance, no, but he figured some sort of warning was due before simply dropping a new employee into the poor man's lap.

Despite the lack of urgency to his letter, it was no surprise when later that same evening, as Henry stood bent over a half-dissected pig on his autopsy table, the cellar door opened and a familiar set of footsteps graced his ears. He didn't even need to look up.

"Good evening, Mr Barker."

"You sent for me," Daniel said. Straight to the point, as always.

Henry had always thought Daniel Barker to be a very fetching young man. One could tell by looking at him he did not come from money, but that he did the best with what he had. Tonight, it meant a well-fitted waistcoat and a freshly pressed shirt, although he'd foregone a tie—as per usual; he detested them. He was almost ridiculously tall, lean, with a head of dark curls and striking blue eyes. Henry was fairly certain the boy's mother had been Jewish, though they did not often speak to one another of their families. Daniel was his friend, perhaps one of his closest, but some topics seemed a touch too personal to broach uninvited.

"I had something I wanted to discuss with you," Henry said, sparing a glance at him before returning his attention to the task at hand. Severing nerves from tissue was an arduous process, one that required steady eyesight and an even steadier hand. "I hired someone to join your crew."

There was a pause, a confused one. "*You* hired someone?"

Henry sincerely hoped that the heat he felt rushing to his face was not visible. "I did."

"Since when do you handle the hiring?" Daniel descended the remaining few steps, stopping on the other side of the autopsy table with his hands in his pockets. Still, Henry refused to look up and meet his eyes.

Why did he feel so ashamed? What did it matter who he employed? So what if he found someone? Except he knew damn well why, in this case. Because he'd been so drawn to that young man, because he found him charming, gentle, funny, attractive.

Henry shoved the thoughts aside and exhaled heavily through his nose. "This was an exception. He needs the work."

"I see." More silence, but he could feel Daniel scrutinising him. "So…you gonna tell me about him?"

"What would you like to know? His name is Lucas Walker. Early twenties, I'd wager. Seems to be of sound mind and body." Almost as quickly as the words left his mouth, Henry flinched, hoping it didn't sound as though it had been a dig at Daniel himself.

If Daniel took it as such, he didn't show it. "Good-lookin', is he?"

Henry's fingers twitched just a fraction to the left, severing a vein he had not meant to sever. His gaze swung sharply up to Daniel's inquisitive face. "I didn't say that—I mean, I hadn't noticed."

"Hm. I'm sure you didn't." A wry smile, bordering on amused, tugged at Daniel's mouth. "Mr Glass, with all due respect, you've got a knack for pitying men who don't deserve your kindness. You realise this about yourself, or else you'd have not left the hiring to me all this time."

He sighed, making no attempt to argue that because Daniel was most certainly correct. "If he doesn't work out, by all means, expel him. Is there harm in giving him a chance?"

It was an unfair question, he realised. Because, yes, there was harm in it. What Daniel did might not have been illegal, *exactly*, but it was still dangerous.

It could still get them caught, get them in trouble, get them injured. All it took was one wrong move, someone losing their nerve, someone spilling information to the authorities…

Daniel met his eyes, chin lifted. And then he looked away. "No, 'course not. So long as you know what you're doing."

Henry felt his expression go sheepish and apologetic. "I'm sorry, Daniel. I know this puts you in an awkward position. I assure you, I would not have suggested someone to this role unless I had the utmost confidence in their character."

"S'fine. Besides, we may be down a man. Barnaby has been missing for the last two weeks. I was about to start hunting for a replacement."

Henry's eyes widened. "Barnaby is missing?"

Daniel turned, examining the specimen jars on the nearby shelf. "No word from him. He didn't show up to the last job."

A frown tugged at Henry's face. Barnaby had been with them for the last year, and of the various men who'd come and gone, he'd been a long-term fixture, of sorts. A friend to Daniel, too, which meant Daniel was no doubt not taking this as well as he appeared. "Was everything all right the last you saw him?"

He shrugged. "Seemed to be. Don't know. He was there, and then he wasn't."

They fell silent, and Henry wished he had something comforting to say, some advice to offer. Something beyond, "I'm certain he's all right. Perhaps one of your connections has seen him."

"Maybe so." Daniel ran a hand back through those impossibly messy curls of his before turning back to Henry. "At any rate, another man along for the ride will be appreciated. Where do I find him?"

"He haunts a pub in the East End by the name of The Rusty Duck."

Daniel's eyebrows shot right up. He had frequented many of the taverns in the East End, once upon a time; it had been outside of one of those pubs that Henry had found him two years prior. "*Really?*"

Now Henry surely was blushing. "Really."

"You not only went to a pub, but you actually chatted someone up? I'm impressed."

"I didn't say I chatted anyone up, Mr Barker."

Daniel folded his arms across his chest. "He chatted *you* up, then? Unsurprising, handsome gent like you."

Henry coughed. "Not…exactly." And when Daniel only stared at him, waiting for him to continue, he had to wonder just why he was incapable of keeping anything from him. It wasn't even that Daniel was pushy or overly inquisitive. Perhaps it was a result of Henry having no one else to speak to.

"He propositioned me," he mumbled after a moment.

Daniel's head tipped slowly. "He wanted to fuck you, and you gave him a job robbing graves."

"Well, I wasn't about to pay him for his bedroom services."

"So, he *was* attractive, then?"

Henry's mouth thinned out. "Perhaps."

He waited for Daniel to needle him, to prod him for more details, but expecting such a thing was really a disservice because that wasn't the sort of man Daniel was. They stared at one another, and all Daniel had to say on the matter was, "I'll be certain to give 'im hell when I meet him, then."

"You're a pain in my arse, Daniel. Are you staying for dinner?"

A slow smile spread across his friend's mouth. "You'd be lost without me, and dinner sounds swell."

SEVEN

Lucas chose not to tell Jasper about his new employment opportunity. Not because he thought his friend would be scandalised—he might have been, just a bit, though he'd never have turned Lucas out for it—but because Jasper was a gentle sort. His profession aside, Jasper was too kind for his own good, too willing to overlook the things people put him through. He was also an honest man, and were anyone to come asking about Lucas, he didn't want to put Jasper in the position of having to lie for his best mate.

Perhaps it was, to some degree, also the fear of something going wrong. As terrified as Lucas was of the whole ordeal, it also seemed too good to be true.

All he needed to do to remind himself that he wasn't dreaming was reach into his pocket to fish out the twenty shillings he'd got the other night.

"Payment in advance," Mr Glass had said, and he'd instructed Lucas to buy himself some new clothes and keep fed until Glass's men sent for him.

He spent that money well, purchasing a fresh pair of boots that weren't falling apart at the soles, an overcoat to protect him from the elements, knowing that perusing cemeteries at night would be cold work, gloves, a shirt, and a pair of trousers. Dressed in his new attire, he made his way to The Rusty Duck with coin to spare in his pocket and a grin on his face. When he found Jasper, Lucas swung his arm around the slighter man and leaned in so he could be heard above the din of conversations.

"Dinner's on me tonight."

Jasper had his dark hair pulled back and braided, though a few strands had fallen loose and hung about his face. He'd never cut it for as long as Lucas had known him, and maybe that was part of what made him so sought after with some of the gents who bought his services. He had a lovely sort of femininity to him, beautiful but handsome. Lucas had seen him in everything from trousers and suits to chemises and corsets. In the right clothing, he'd have had little trouble passing as a woman.

His eyes widened as he leaned back and looked Lucas over. "Well, look at you. Did you—"

"Land meself a job? Sure did." He puffed out his chest with a pleased smirk. "But I can't tell you what it is. At least not yet."

Smiling, Jasper reached out to touch admiring fingers to the lapels of Lucas's new overcoat. "You sure? About dinner, I mean."

"Positive." Lucas caught him by the hand and led him through the tavern to snag a spot in time for the next round of meals to be served.

Dinner would not be a fanciful affair—pork pies, fish, a bit of pudding, and a glass of gin—but it filled their bellies, and Lucas was proud that he could pay for the first time in ages. Jasper, never one for large meals, seemed delighted with the pudding and ate that before even looking at the rest.

Hours later, they walked back to The Sun and Stars with Lucas singing merrily while wobbling on his feet and Jasper—startlingly with his wits about him despite how much he'd also had to drink—laughing and helping to steady Lucas before he could tip over.

They stopped outside the front doors. Lucas glared at a man who shoved past them exiting the building, and Jasper touched his arm to refocus his attention. Lucas swung his gaze back to him with a smile. "Tonight was good, yeah?"

"It was." Jasper smiled, but there was an edge of uncertainty in his tone and at the corners of his eyes.

Lucas frowned. "But…?"

"But I just… Are you sure it was all right? You haven't told me a thing about this new job all night."

He crammed his hands into his pockets and cast his eyes skyward. "I told you, it's just gotta be a little quiet for now."

Jasper tucked his lower lip between his teeth and drew in a slow breath. Lucas knew that look. It was his *you're worrying me, but I don't want to be a bother* look. "The only reason you ever hide things from me is when you know I'll disapprove."

"It ain't that." Although it was. Sort of. A little bit. "I just don't wanna risk it in case somethin' falls through, y'know? My luck's been shit for so long, and it might finally be turning around." Lucas brought his hands to Jasper's shoulders and squeezed. "Everything's gonna be fine, and that's what's important, right?"

"I trust you." The corners of Jasper's eyes crinkled faintly when he smiled, and Lucas knew that he'd won—at least for now. Who knew how long he could keep this secret? "Do you need to sneak in tonight? Sounds pretty quiet in there."

"Nah, weather's not too bad." Lucas drew back and adjusted his greatcoat, pleased with the warmth it provided. That, coupled with the alcohol in his system, would stave off the chill for at least a little while. "Before much longer, I'll have myself a nice flat all my own. Then maybe you can come stay with me sometimes, just to get away."

Jasper chuckled and took a step for the door, though something about the way he diverted his gaze felt…off, as though he doubted that would happen. "Good night, Lu."

He disappeared inside, leaving Lucas with a lingering sense of unease and bewilderment in his gut.

Three days later, Francis, the owner of The Rusty Duck, handed Lucas a note that had been dropped off for him earlier that day. It was not written in any sort of elegant scrawl he would have expected from Henry Glass, so he suspected it was from one of the men in his employ.

8 p.m.

Calvary Cemetery

east entrance

Any appetite he might have had for dinner vanished. He'd known this day was coming. He'd been living off that money from Glass, and now it was time to go out and earn it.

There's more where that came from, he reminded himself. *Steady on. You've got this.*

He managed to eat half a pork pie and down a glass of ale before setting off on his way. It placed him at the east entrance of the cemetery thirty minutes early, and he lingered in the dark behind a row of trees by the gates, quietly praying he wouldn't be spotted by any guards who might've been posted on watch.

After what felt like hours but was only thirty minutes, the soft sound of steps on the path leading up to the gates reached his ears. He tensed, stole a look around the tree, and spotted two men headed his way.

Although it was dark, he could make out the shapes of shovels and canvas bags on their persons amid the mild light of a swinging lantern from one man's hand, and it wasn't until he stepped into their line of sight that it occurred to him they might be body snatchers but maybe not *the* body snatchers he was waiting for.

Thankfully, one of the men lifted a hand in greeting when they were close enough to be heard. "Walker, is it?"

"Yeah, s'right." He was also suddenly aware that he'd not been told what their names were—and that he'd anticipated three of them, not two. Lucas squared his shoulders and lifted his chin, overly aware of his fairly short stature, and given that this bloke was impressively tall, it only accentuated the height difference.

The tall bloke tipped his head down as they stopped at the gates. He offered a hand, which Lucas took; it was calloused and rough, perhaps from long months or even years of this type of work. He wasn't bad-looking, all things considered—blue eyes, dark curly hair that he'd maybe attempted to tame earlier in the day. Something in the way he presented himself suggested he was older than he appeared. Late twenties, early thirties, if Lucas had to guess.

"Daniel Barker," the man introduced himself and then nodded to the stocky, red-haired, freckled man behind him that looked not much older than Lucas was. "This is Allen Pendleton."

Lucas crammed his hands into his pockets and sniffed from the cold, bobbing his head into a nod. "Pleasure, gents."

Barker smiled as though at some private joke or perhaps at being referred to as a gentleman despite what they were about to do. "It's your first time, yeah? Just follow our lead, do what you're told, and you'll be fine."

Brilliant, Lucas thought. He could follow their lead.

And follow he did. Barker led them along the crude fence surrounding the cemetery, coming to a spot amidst a cluster of trees, where he stopped and handed the shovels he carried to Pendleton and then squeezed his way through a gap in the fence. On the other side, he turned around and reached back through to take the tools, and only then did Pendleton follow him.

Lucas bit his lip. This was his last chance to go back. Last chance to change his mind.

He closed his eyes, took a deep breath, and slipped through after the others.

The three of them crept through the cemetery grounds, picking through overgrown grass and weeds and unkempt graves. Lucas's curiosity got the best of him, and he picked up the pace to fall in line with Daniel Barker.

"There's s'posed to be four of us, yeah?"

"Lost a man. More money for the rest of us."

"Oh." He paused. "What good's a fence, if it don't keep no one out?"

Barker glanced at him. "Imagine it deters some folks from tryin', but we've worked this place before precisely because it's easy. No towers, no stone walls, rarely any guards."

"Why's that?"

"Can't you tell? Look around. No one gives a damn about the graves here." He shrugged, switching his shovel from one shoulder to the other. "Most we might encounter here is a relative or two guarding the graves of the recently deceased, and even that's rare."

Lucas stole a glance around. It was true, and it was a bit depressing when he thought about it. This was the sort of place people with no money or social status came to when they died. People like Barker and Pendleton.

People like him and Jasper.

They cleared a good two-thirds of the cemetery before coming upon a grave with dirt freshly placed and a tombstone only recently set. Lucas halted when the others did. Pendleton raised the lantern to the headstone to check the name.

"Mortimer Crandle. This is it," he said. He turned to Lucas and pushed a shovel into his hands. "We take turns digging. It's your first night, so you get to start us off."

Lucas looked down at the shovel, heart pounding a mile a minute. The body was barely cold in the ground, and they'd be disturbing it. If this man had any family to mourn him, they'd be crying over a patch of empty dirt.

But this dead man also meant Lucas would eat for the next week or two.

He began to dig.

He worked until his back throbbed and his shoulders burned, piling dirt off to the side, and shrugged Barker off the first time he offered for them to switch. Lucas was determined to show he could pull his own weight. Or perhaps he wanted to do more digging in hopes of getting out of whatever else needed to be done.

When he finally grew too sore and exhausted, sweating enough that he had discarded his overcoat, he let Pendleton take over. It was during Barker's turn that the unmistakable sound of metal striking wood sent a shudder down Lucas's spine.

The hole they'd dug was not, in fact, even the full length of the coffin. Just a square close to the headstone. Barker pressed his back against the side of the hole, braced himself, and drove the shovel down. Once, and then again, and again, until the lid of the coffin began to splinter and give.

Lucas stared in morbid fascination as Barker crouched to pry the remaining loose planks away, revealing the head and shoulders of the corpse at rest within. He hauled himself from the grave, tossing the shovel aside.

To Lucas's horror, Barker turned to him and nodded. "Go on then. Get him out of there."

Damned good thing he'd not had much of a dinner or else he'd have lost it just then. He looked to Pendleton, whose gaze was elsewhere, likely on the lookout, and then to the open grave. "How do I…"

"Just get in there, grab 'im beneath the arms, and pull. Easier than unearthing the entire damn grave; we don't have time for that." Barker dusted off his hands and rolled his shoulders. "Get to it."

His insides a jumbled mess, Lucas approached the edge of the hole and began to lower himself in. He braced his feet upon the outer edges of the coffin, afraid they'd give way and send him crashing right down onto Mr Mortimer Crandle.

At that moment, a lot of things came to him at once. Like the smell, which was not pleasant, to say the least. Or the horror of the situation, that he was desecrating a grave, and that he didn't know if he believed in an afterlife or a Heaven, but, if there was a God, He would surely frown at this.

Or the sensation of his skin crawling as he crouched down and held his breath and hooked his arms beneath Mr Crandle's and heaved with all his strength.

It was dead weight. Literally. He strained until the body began to move, pushed up with his legs until they trembled, and managed to get to standing. Barker was right there, knelt at the edge of the gravesite, ready to grab hold of the corpse's arm and help to haul him out onto level ground. Lucas gratefully scrambled out after him.

He flopped back onto the dewy grass to catch his breath and still his quaking hands. Pendleton set to stripping Crandle down, everything from his clothes to a St. Christopher's medal round his neck, and tossing it all back into the coffin. Lucas recalled what Mr Glass had said: stealing a person's body wasn't illegal, but stealing their belongings was.

They wrapped the body back in its shroud. Barker called for Lucas to help him get Crandle stuffed into one of the canvas sacks he'd brought while Pendleton began to refill the grave.

They left the cemetery with one more than they'd entered with.

Thankfully, Mortimer Crandle had not been a heavy man. It made transporting him through the fence opening easier than it otherwise would have been and the trip down the pathway to the road faster. Lucas had wondered if they were supposed to carry the damned thing all the way to Glass's and felt relief when Barker brought them to a horse and wagon on the street.

They deposited Crandle into an empty box, which was not particularly long and rather square in shape, which meant they had to fold the dead man up to make him fit.

"Less conspicuous," Pendleton explained. "In case we get stopped."

They covered the box with a tarp, loaded it into the cart, and set off.

Lucas slumped into the back of the wagon while Pendleton drove. Barker joined him after a spell, offering out a flask, which Lucas took a swig from without question.

"All right?" Barker asked.

"Yeah. Yeah, fine." Lucas offered back the flask with a sigh.

The other man nodded once and clapped him on the back. "Congratulations, mate. You just snatched your first body. You're a resurrectionist now."

EIGHT

They rolled up to the back of Mr Glass's house close to midnight, dirty, tired, and having barely spoken a word to one another. Lucas didn't have it in him to be social and inquire more about either of his companions, and they didn't come across as the chatty sorts who had any interest in small talk anyway.

When the wagon came to a stop, Barker hopped out and rapped his knuckles three times on the back door. A moment later, it swung open, and Mr Glass appeared.

Lucas thought he saw the surgeon scanning their faces before settling on him, as though Glass had been looking specifically for him. When their eyes met, Glass smiled, and Lucas's exhaustion seemed to clear as he flashed a grin in return.

He and Pendleton carted the box into what ought to have been an ordinary cellar but instead had been converted into an autopsy room complete with gurneys and tables, jars upon the shelves filled with liquid and—when Lucas ventured closer to have a look—organs and animals and many things he wasn't sure he wanted to identify. At one point, he found himself face-to-face with a mass of brain tissue behind glass, and he barely bit back the compulsion to ask if it had belonged to a human or not.

When he turned back around, Glass had the box open and was having a look at Mr Crandle's body.

"Good. Excellent," he murmured, more to himself than any of them. "Well done, gentlemen. Can I interest you in a warm drink for your troubles?"

"Money'll do just fine, sir," Pendleton grunted, already looking impatient to take his leave.

Glass smiled sombrely and procured from his pocket a handful of coins, which he began to stack in three piles upon the autopsy table next to Mr Crandle. "I notice we're still missing Barnaby."

"Not so sure we'll be seeing him again," Barker murmured, dropping his eyes to the money.

Glass gave pause at that, glancing up. "Daniel?"

Barker shrugged. "Got caught with his prick in the wrong arse this time, I guess."

The room fell silent, and Lucas looked between the three men, at a loss to what was going on. Glass quietly doled out the remaining coins, offering Barker and Pendleton their share, which they took with acknowledging nods and swiftly pocketed. They left not a moment later, not even asking if Lucas wanted a ride to—well, anywhere. Surely wherever they were headed was closer to his stamping grounds than was Glass's place.

The door swung shut behind them, and Glass sighed, picking up the remaining coins and offering them out to Lucas with a smile. "No complaints from them. Well done. You've earned this."

Lucas tucked the money into his pocket, savouring the weight of it there, knowing what it would mean for him in the days to come. "A pleasure."

"Could I trouble you to assist me for a moment?"

Lucas stepped forward to help him get Crandle out of the box and laid out on the autopsy table. Afterwards, he rubbed his hands against his trousers, grateful he'd not worn his new ones. He felt like he'd be scrubbing away the smell of death for weeks.

Glass began to unravel the shroud, performing a thorough examination of Crandle's body, until he came across what he appeared to be searching for—an immense, malformed lump upon the man's abdomen. Some sort of unnatural growth Lucas couldn't have named, but it was grotesquely impressive, all the same.

Studying Glass, Lucas readjusted the cap upon his head. "Well, I ought to be getting back."

"Back where?" Glass asked absently, not looking up. "Have you found someplace to stay?"

"I've been renting a room at The Rusty Duck."

"Ah. Well, the offer for a warm drink remains, if you aren't in a hurry."

He swallowed hard, wondering if that invitation was meant to be taken at face value—as nothing more than an offer for tea—or if Glass had some ulterior motive. It was true, he had no reason to rush back to The Rusty Duck just yet. His room wasn't going anywhere. It would be a long, cold walk, and his hands were numb and blistered from the last few hours outside.

"A drink sounds all right," he said.

Glass led him up the stairs and into the house. His dog sat in the kitchen waiting for them, immediately jumping at Lucas's legs for attention until he stooped to pick it—her, by the looks of it—up. Glass cast him an amused look over his shoulder.

"She likes you. She doesn't usually warm up to people so quickly."

"Always been good with dogs." Lucas scratched behind the terrier's alert ears. The feel of wiry fur certainly took him back; the dogs he'd worked with as a child had been the only thing keeping him from losing his way in the dark. Maybe they hadn't been good conversationalists, but they'd been good listeners. "She got a name?"

"Hilda." Glass led him back to the parlour where they'd shared a drink the week before. Lucas helped himself to the same seat, letting Hilda settle in his lap where she stayed still so long as he continued to pet her.

It seemed Glass had been in the middle of pouring himself tea when Lucas and the others had arrived. The older man filled two cups and brought the tea cart closer. Lucas didn't even bother with sugar for his. He took the warm cup and brought it to his lips, enjoying the heat flooding into his fingers and the steam wafting into his airways.

For a bit, they remained quiet, but it was not an uncomfortable sort of silence. Lucas was exhausted, and Mr Glass seemed all right letting him bask by the fire and enjoy his drink.

It was only after Glass had finished his cup and gone to pour a second that he said, "You haven't told me how you fared tonight."

Lucas opened his eyes, which had begun to droop shut the longer the warmth and lethargy settled into his bones. "Said it yourself, didn't you? No complaints from them."

"I meant how *you* were feeling about the ordeal, not what they thought of your performance."

That was a hard question. Lucas sipped at his tea, relishing that it was still almost hot enough to scald going down. "Can't say it was loads of fun or nothin', but I can handle it, if that's what you're wonderin'."

Glass smiled. "I never had any doubts that you could. Just whether or not you'd *want* to—and whether you'd like to continue doing it on a regular basis."

Lucas looked down at Hilda, whose back leg twitched in the throes of a dream. With money in his pocket, he could hop a train and leave London. He could go to any other city, maybe somewhere up north, and land himself a factory job where no one knew who he was. If he was careful, he'd have enough funds to pay for the trip, a few more new items of clothing, and a bit of rent for a flat somewhere.

Except he circled back around to the same issues as before. Namely, leaving the city he knew as his home. Leaving Jasper. Being the way that he was, there was comfort to be had knowing he had others just like him. A whole little community, in fact.

He looked back at Mr Glass. "No long-term promises, but for now I can keep on. Seems like you're short a bloke now, anyway, yeah?"

The other man's smile faltered a little. "It would appear that way."

"What'd Barker mean? About what he got in trouble for."

Glass sighed, lifting his cup to his lips and hesitating before taking a sip. "The dangers of being a man who fancies other men, Mr Walker. When one gets caught, it tends to upset one's life."

A long pause before the meaning of that properly sunk in. "He was—like us?"

"Like us," Glass agreed. "Barnaby was not a terribly careful lad. Once, a few men caught him engaged with another gentleman in an alley somewhere and left him nearly for dead in a gutter. Mr Barker found him and brought him onto the crew after he recovered."

"Sorry," Lucas found himself murmuring. "If you two were...friends or whatever."

"On friendly enough terms, I suppose, though I'm not certain you'd say *friends*. He was my worker. Mr Barker was closer with him, however. I suspect he's not taking this as well as he appeared to be."

That led to the question of whether Daniel Barker also shared their preferences for men. And Pendleton, for that matter. He thought to ask as much, if all the people Glass had gathered for this little project were of the same persuasion. Clearly, Barker *knew*, at the very least.

But Glass had his gaze on the fireplace, a look of melancholy stretched across his features, and Lucas thought it might be better to keep his nosiness in check for the time being. He downed the remainder of his tea and gently began to coax Hilda off his lap.

"Thanks for the drink. I ought to be heading out."

Glass's gaze slid slowly back to him. "You'll be hard-pressed to find a cab at this hour."

"I can walk."

"You'll be lucky to get home by sunrise, then."

Lucas scoffed. "Got a better idea for me?"

A pause. "You could stay here."

They stared at one another, and Lucas thought his host looked just as startled that the offer had left his own mouth as Lucas was.

"Sorry, yeah, you...want me to stay here? With you? Or..." He moved to the edge of his seat, trying to get a proper read of the situation. Was it a proposition? Did a man just invite another man to stay over under these circumstances? Maybe they did. It wasn't like Lucas would have any idea how that all worked. For as tired as he was, the thought was enough to perk him right up.

But Henry Glass gave him a wry little smile and arched his eyebrows. "I have a guest room you may use, if it pleases you."

Lucas deflated back into his seat, trying to mask his disappointment. Maybe his embarrassment too, for having jumped to conclusions. "Yeah, all right. Thanks."

They finished off their drinks, and Glass led the way upstairs. His butler, Frederick, had long since gone to bed, Glass explained. It seemed cruel to wake him just to show Lucas to his room.

And what a room it was.

Lucas stepped inside, gaping at the wide stretch of floor space and the heavy, embroidered draperies. The bed was nearly as wide as it was long, and he wanted nothing more than to fall face-first into it and sleep for a year.

As it was, it occurred to him how dirty his work had left him and that he didn't want to ruin the clean bedclothes. When Glass left the room, he immediately began to yank off his coat and peel out of his shirt. Glass returned in short order with a jug of water for washing up, and he paused when he laid eyes on Lucas, who also stilled, colour rising to his face.

Glass cleared his throat and turned to place the jug atop the wash table, along with a folded garment Lucas suspected was a nightgown. He'd been sleeping in the nude during his time at The Rusty Duck, but only because he didn't have any nightclothes of his own.

"I'll request Frederick draw you a proper bath in the morning. This will have to do for now."

Lucas rubbed his bare arms, offering a crooked grin. "Good bit a' hospitality. You do this for all your new employees?"

"Only the pretty ones." Glass returned the smile briefly.

It would have been a wasted opportunity if Lucas didn't take that comment and run with it. His grin turned sultry, and he leaned into the dresser with a pleased tip of his head. "S'that right? And here I'd begun to think I wasn't your type."

He caught the way Glass looked at him, the way the other man's warm hazel eyes raked over his bare torso and up again to settle upon his face—and how he then swiftly glanced away before their gazes could meet. Lucas wanted him to look back, to look at him, to give some sort of sign that Lucas ought to approach and show him just how grateful he was.

"I've work in the morning," Glass finally said, although his tone was a touch lower than it'd been a moment ago. "Please get some rest. Good night, Mr Walker."

He took his leave, shutting the door as he went. Lucas heaved a disappointed sigh. Glass was no good at taking a bloody hint, and *he* wasn't so great at giving them to begin with.

Or else Lucas had misread something, and the man wasn't the least bit interested. Perhaps he truly was only trying to be kind.

He turned to the washbowl, filled it from the jug, dunked his hands into the chilly water, and scrubbed rigorously at his face. It was no more than he'd have got back at his own room, but it felt nicer somehow. He took his time stripping the rest of the way down and washing up until he felt clean enough to pull on the borrowed nightgown and fall into bed.

The bedclothes smelled floral and sweet and fresh, but there was something that reached his senses he couldn't quite pinpoint at first. Not until he happened to lift an arm to the pillow beside his face and caught the scent of his sleeve. He nestled his nose into the fabric and breathed in deep. It had that same aroma of cleanliness to it, but beneath that—the smell of cologne or aftershave.

The nightgown smelled like Henry Glass.

Lucas closed his eyes. This little schoolboy crush of his was bordering on obnoxious. That he couldn't even lie in a bed without thinking that the man was just a few doors down, likely undressing for the night, and imagining what might happen if he got up and marched down there and let himself into Glass's room...

Fuckin' mad, is what you are, he scolded himself, not without a soft laugh against his pillow.

If nothing else, he could slip a hand beneath the blankets, between his legs, and allow his imagination to run away with him.

Just for tonight.

NINE

Lucas woke with an abundance of sore muscles and stiff limbs, though he was not altogether uncomfortable despite it. The pain was a result of the laborious work the night before, but the bed was warm and soft and he woke slowly instead of all at once as he often did. One learned to rise early and quickly when one slept out in the open, and, even at The Rusty Duck, Lucas often startled awake to the sound of doors slamming or men's voices in adjacent rooms. No one cared enough to be quiet.

Years of such things meant he still stirred early even in the comfort and safety of Henry Glass's home, but he reminded himself he had no cause to get out of bed just yet. Instead, he nestled further beneath the blankets, breathing in deeply.

How nice it must be, he thought, *to live like this.* To have comfort and security every night, to never wonder when it might be ripped out from under you.

What eventually coaxed him out of bed was the rumbling of his stomach, reminding him he'd not managed much of a dinner the night before. He splashed cold water on his face, catching the tail end of footsteps out in the hall, soft but purposeful, and opened the door to poke his head out.

The butler, Frederick, turned towards the sound. "Good morning, Mr Walker. Did you have a good sleep?"

"Fantastic." He rubbed a hand back over his sleep-tousled hair and grinned. "What time is it?"

"Just a quarter 'til seven, sir. We'd not expected you to be up for quite some time."

"Always been an early riser."

"So it would seem. Would you like me to have a bath readied for you?"

A part of Lucas had no interest in imposing on Glass's household further, but when would he get this sort of chance again? The baths at The Rusty Duck were expensive, ice-cold, and often with well water that looked and smelled a little suspect, and while there were public bathhouses... Maybe he could enjoy himself, just this once. "If it ain't too much trouble."

Frederick instructed him to come downstairs in short order. Lucas ducked back into his room and went to the window, nudging the curtains aside to have a look. It was raining out. Brilliant. He'd be walking home in that.

Nah, mate. You can ride home in that. Cabs were a luxury he could rarely afford, but indulging in it occasionally wouldn't be all that bad, would it?

He went downstairs as instructed and found Frederick waiting for him in the hall. The butler led him to a dedicated bathroom across from the kitchens, where he was left with a towel and a set of fresh clothes.

"From Master Glass," Frederick said.

He shut the door and left Lucas there. Steam rolled off the water's surface, and a small table set to the side was adorned with soaps and oils, a sponge, a flat razor, and a mirror. All that, coupled with the new clothes, left Lucas teetering a little off-kilter. He wasn't used to this level of kindness.

He undressed, letting his clothes drop carelessly to the floor, and slid into the tub with a hiss through gritted teeth. Heat seeped into every scratch and cut he hadn't realised he possessed, teased at his tense muscles, and began to lick away the pain.

God, but he'd have loved to stay in there all day, if only the water would keep warm. As it was, he remained for a long while in the steamy little room, head tipped back against the edge of the tub and simply soaking. When he moved, it was to draw the table closer to him and pick through the various soaps to scrub his body properly, thoroughly clean for the first time in what felt like ages, and to shave.

By the time he finished with all that, the water had begun to cool, now tepid but still comfortable. Reluctantly Lucas stepped out of the tub, dried off, and turned to the new clothes.

The first thing that caught him off guard was the quality. Better than anything he'd ever owned by far. The second was that, as he pulled on the clothes, they fit surprisingly well. He'd thought maybe Mr Glass had some spare items lying around, but these fit so well that Lucas couldn't help but wonder if they'd been bought specifically for him and with his measurements in mind.

He turned to the full-length mirror in the corner and swiped the towel across the steamed-over glass.

Hardly recognize meself dressed like a proper gent, he thought in amusement, smoothing a hand down the front of his shirt and waistcoat. *This* was what he ought to have shown up wearing that night for supper. This made him look like he was someone important, someone who mattered.

That thought was bittersweet. Truly, he was no different a person than he'd been a few hours ago, dressed in his own bedraggled clothes. But if he were to go out like this, he wondered... How would the world look at him then? Would he be greeted differently by those he passed on the street? By shop owners and potential employers? Would society suddenly think him worthy of respect and kindness, just because he dressed above his station?

With a sigh and a hand shoved back through his damp hair, Lucas turned away, trying to shake the feeling that he didn't belong in this house or in these clothes.

Much to his surprise, Frederick had breakfast laid out for him when he emerged from the bathing room. More surprising yet, the table was set for two, and Mr Glass was seated and waiting for him.

"I thought you'd have left already," Lucas said.

Glass looked up. His eyes widened a bit as he gave Lucas an appraising once-over before his expression smoothed out again. "I thought I might enjoy a proper meal before work. I also thought we might ride together. The hospital is a bit closer to your neighbourhood, isn't it?"

"Yeah, it is." Lucas took a seat, tugging at the collar of his shirt self-consciously. "Um. Thank you, by the by. For all of this. The bath and the clothes."

Glass reached for his fork, cracking a smile. "Think nothing of it. I'm pleased my estimates of your measurements were acceptable."

"Not bad, actually." He tugged at the sleeves, which were a smidge too long, but nothing he couldn't deal with.

"Excellent." Glass set his fork aside and leaned back, watching Lucas as though debating whether to speak further.

Lucas paused. "What is it?"

"If you are not in any hurry," Glass began slowly, "I thought we might make a stop along the way and have your measurements taken properly?"

He blinked, looking down at himself. "What's wrong with how they fit now? I don't need to get 'em tailored."

"Even so, it would be better to have accurate numbers so I might get you a few more things?"

Their eyes met across the table, Lucas frowning in bewilderment and Glass looking as though he was having trouble not dropping his gaze to his plate.

"Why would you wanna do that?" Lucas asked.

"After seeing what you wore to supper the other night, I thought it might be beneficial for you to have something…" He trailed off, waving his hand in a helpless gesture. No doubt none of the words coming to mind were particularly flattering.

Lucas frowned. "Something *what?*"

"Something…newer."

A small flicker of embarrassment reared its head. "I don't need your charity."

"Consider it part of your payment, Mr Walker. I did it because I wanted to, not because I thought you needed it."

Just like that, the flicker was extinguished. Glass looked so crestfallen and unsure of himself that Lucas regretted having scolded him over it. But damned if he wasn't confused as hell, trying to figure out this man who was so kind to him but who shied away any time Lucas tried to get physically closer.

He looked down at his clothes, smoothing a hand down the buttons of his coat, admiring the fine stitching. "It *does* look quite fetching on me, don't it?"

Glass lifted his chin with a hesitant smile. "You look very fine, Mr Walker."

"When are you gonna start calling me Lucas?"

"I do not see you calling me by my Christian name, either."

Lucas crammed a bite of scone into his mouth, realised it was probably far too large a bite to be proper and made quick work of chewing and swallowing. "That's 'cause you're… I mean, you're older. And distinguished. And a surgeon." *And well-off, and I spend most of my nights in a fuckin' gutter.*

"I think if you're going to expect me to use your given name, as though we are equals, I can request the same in return." He raised an eyebrow at Lucas, who frowned again, and clearly, they were at an impasse because neither of them was willing to bend. Lucas shoved a defiant bite of food into his mouth, and that ended the argument—though hardly solved it—for the time being.

After they'd finished their meal and made last-minute preparations, Glass escorted him outside to a waiting cab. It was a step above the rickety old wagon he'd ridden in the night before. The enclosed carriage kept out the worst of the chilly weather, although Lucas found his new jacket did quite a good job of keeping him warm as well.

Mostly, though, he was distinctly aware of Henry Glass beside him, close enough he could have shifted just so and they'd have been touching. The silence was not an uncomfortable one, but Lucas struggled for words to fill it all the same.

Although he hadn't officially given his agreement to stop anywhere, the cab did come to a halt long before they reached the hospital. When they disembarked, a tailor shop stood before them. Certainly nicer than any Lucas had ever been in; he was very grateful to already be wearing something better than his usual attire, and to have bathed.

Glass escorted him inside where a seamstress greeted them with a smile.

"Mr Glass, lovely to see you."

"Mrs Nicholls." Glass placed a hand flat against Lucas's back, and Lucas stood up a little straighter. "This is Mr Walker, a good friend of mine. I'd like to see about getting his measurements taken and having you make a few things for him."

"Of course." She turned that kind smile to Lucas and beckoned him along into the back of the shop.

For the next twenty minutes, he stood with his legs apart and arms outstretched to either side of him while Mrs Nicholls and a young assistant— her daughter, perhaps, Lucas thought they looked alike—ran a measuring tape along his limbs and about his middle, jotting down numbers as they went. It was a swift and efficient process during which Lucas didn't say a word because no one really acknowledged him as needing to be spoken to, and he didn't want to interrupt their work.

Afterwards, he returned to Glass, who'd been busying himself flipping through illustrations in a catalogue. To Mrs Nicholls, he pointed out a few things, and Lucas craned his neck to try to see what, exactly, was being purchased for him. A few shirts, a few pairs of trousers, socks, undergarments even—which made Lucas blush a little when Mrs Nicholls smiled and winked in his direction.

"Would you like to settle the bill on pickup?" Mrs Nicholls asked.

"Please. Come along, Mr Walker." Glass bid the women a good day and ushered Lucas outside. Lucas glanced back only once, wishing he'd got a quick look at the write-up to see just what sort of money Glass had dropped on him.

"Don't know how much all that just cost you, but—"

"As I said, part of your payment."

The footman opened their door, and Glass urged Lucas in first. Once he'd settled into the relative warmth of the carriage once more, he levelled a frown at his companion. He truly doubted Glass went through all this effort for any of his other workers. "I don't get a say in this?"

Glass paused. "Are you displeased?"

"I'm not..." Sigh. "I'm not *displeased*. I just don't get why you're doin' all this. There's no reason for it." It came out a bit more forceful than Lucas had intended, and for half a second, Glass seemed taken aback. But then he smiled, a faint, ghostly sort of smile that didn't quite reach his eyes, and he merely turned to look out the window.

Lucas slumped back into his seat. He didn't for a second think that Glass was doing it for any reason other than out of the kindness of his heart, and it was true that the clothing would be beneficial to him, but it was discomforting. Lucas hated handouts. From strangers, from Jasper, from Mr Glass... He wanted to be an independent, self-sufficient man, not someone who only got by with the mercy of others.

The silence began to get to him after a spell.

"Any idea when you'll need me again?" he finally asked once the streets began to look familiar to him, suggesting they were nearing their destination.

Glass, who'd been watching the scenery go by, glanced at him. "Next week, likely. It depends on how this particular autopsy goes."

"Oh. Right." Not that far away, and yet it felt like ages. He fidgeted. "So, you cut 'im up and stuff him in those jars on your shelves?"

Glass chuckled. Lucas loved the way his eyes crinkled when he did that.

"That's a possibility, yes, but not always. Mr Crandle died from that tumour you saw on his abdomen. I had tried to encourage him to allow me to operate while he was alive, but tumour removal is…well, tricky. Another of my colleagues talked him out of it."

"Why the hell would he do that?"

"Some men are resistant to change, Mr Walker. Including, or perhaps especially, many in the medical field. They're so afraid of risks that they'd rather allow their patients to die slow and painful deaths than to take a chance that they can save them—or prolong their lives, at the very least."

"Huh. Were you mad about it?"

"Not particularly. To each his own. Were you in Mr Crandle's position, what would you have done?"

Lucas tipped his head back, considering. If he were ill and a surgeon thought they could save him, but there was a chance he could die during the procedure, would he do it? Or would he live out the remainder of his life as best as he was able? "I think…I ain't ready to die. And livin' like that ain't really no way to live. If you were the surgeon who thought he could save me, I'd trust you to do it."

The cab rolled to a stop and, Lucas realised, it had brought them all the way back to his own neighbourhood, just a block or two from The Rusty Duck.

Glass gave him a smile full of light and softness that Lucas had not seen before. "Thank you for saying so, Lucas."

The sound of his name on the other man's lips made him warm all the way down to his toes. He grinned despite himself, awkward and ridiculously shy, and reached up to fidget with his cap. "Yeah, well. I'll see you 'round. Thanks for the ride and—you know. Everythin'."

He opened the door and climbed out, stepping from one world back into another. As Glass's cab rumbled away down the cobblestone street, Lucas watched him go. All the colour in the world seemed to go with him.

TEN

"Three shillings a week," the old man said.

Lucas cast a dubious look about the flat. The roof clearly had a few leaks, the outdoor privy was shared with at least four other families in the courtyard, and the windows had broken panes of glass.

He pursed his lips. "Seems a bit pricey…"

Mr Koffner squinted. "Then find somethin' else."

Except there *was* nothing else. Not in this neighbourhood, at least. If he went much further west, the rents leapt sky-high. He couldn't afford to keep sleeping at The Rusty Duck, and he wanted his own space. Besides that, all he needed was somewhere to call his own for a few weeks. He could keep looking for something better in the meantime.

With a sigh, Lucas fished a few coins from his pocket and offered them out. "Couple of weeks in advance. That all right?"

Koffner scratched his dirty nails across his grizzled chin and swiped the money. Then he tossed the key to Lucas, turned, and walked out. The door groaned shut in his wake.

Lucas dropped his rucksack and took a seat on the straw mattress in the corner. He wouldn't be surprised if the damn thing was infested with lice and fleas, though the cold weather might help take care of both. There was no insulation either, which meant the nights were going to be brutal and he'd need to purchase himself some blankets when he got paid again. Until then, he hoped the little wood-burning stove would do well enough to heat the small space.

Still, it was his. No more hauling his belongings around or stashing them at Jasper's place. For that matter, maybe he could coax Jasper to get out occasionally, to come have dinner here with him. He had the stove, a small table near the window, and he could get a hold of some dishes cheaply enough.

All he had on his person were the clothes he'd worn body-snatching—which he currently wore—and the outfit Glass had bought for him. That, he tucked away with care into an old dresser near the foot of the bed, where the last occupant of the place had left behind some dirty socks and a belt and a child's dress. He collected those things and put them outside, figuring one of the neighbours might find some use for them.

After reorganising some of the meagre furniture in his new flat, Lucas ducked back outside, locked the door behind him, waved cheerfully to a woman hanging laundry just across the way, and loped out of the courtyard and down the street. His first stop was The Sun and Stars, but Miss Beatrice scolded him and turned him out, saying Jasper had no time for guests, so off he went by himself to market.

He didn't know much about cooking, really. He'd always eaten what he could get a hold of. Even when he'd lived on his own before, he'd survived largely off poorly made potato stew, eggs, and bread. Which were staples he purchased now too, just in case, but he also allowed himself a few things he'd not had in some time. A couple of ears of corn, some apples and fish and ginger beer, and some chestnuts that would come in handy when he needed to eat on the go for work. He also stopped by the general store and got himself some dishes, a second-hand blanket, and a cookbook.

It was dark out by the time he returned home, and he was too tired to make the trek back to The Sun and Stars. He put up his food, got a fire going in the stove, and collapsed into bed. The air was cold and wet, the flat smelled funny, and his stomach rumbled, but he was too tired to care—and maybe it was easier, going hungry, when he knew there was food at hand if he really wanted it.

He drifted off to sleep with a smile on his face.

It wasn't much, but it was his.

ELEVEN

It'd been four days since Lucas had seen Mr Glass, and five days since he'd seen Jasper. Madam Beatrice still turned him away anytime he stopped by. There was no sign of him at The Rusty Duck, either, and that in and of itself was troubling. Although Jasper did much of his work at The Sun and Stars, he often showed up at The Duck for extra funds, particularly on Fridays. Drunk men were much easier to overcharge, Lucas suspected, and Beatrice took a good chunk of the proceeds anyone made under her roof. He couldn't recall the last time Jasper had missed a Friday—the day most men got paid. Busiest day at The Duck.

Lucas ate dinner there and left early after only a drink or two and headed to The Sun and Stars. It was late, and the place would be teeming with culls, so he scaled the neighbouring roof and leaned across to knock instead—only after listening to ensure he wasn't interrupting anything. He hoped.

No answer.

Fuck, c'mon, Jasper.

He knocked again, louder, worry starting to edge into his chest. Beatrice wouldn't have kept it from him if something had gone wrong, right? She'd have told him if Jasper was sick?

Likely not, the old bat's got it in for me.

Lucas waited a few minutes before knocking one last time. When he was greeted with silence, he reluctantly retreated from his perch, lingering in the alley below and pacing circles while he tried to think of what to do.

He could try begging an answer off Beatrice again. Hell, maybe he could offer to pay for an hour of Jasper's time just to get in there to see him. The more he thought about it, the better an idea it sounded, so he circled around to the front of the building and let himself inside.

Really, The Sun and Stars looked like any house, though it aimed for looking like one of those high-class escort establishments and fell quite short of it. He'd heard from men at the Duck that some of the East End whorehouses, although fewer and further between, were decorated as finely as any manor house. This house could've used a good scrubbing from top to bottom, and when one looked closely and noticed where the wallpaper was peeling, and the banisters were chipped and in need of re-staining, and the rugs were worn through in places, it became apparent The Sun and Stars wasn't as nice as Beatrice played it off to be.

Several of the girls lounged about in the parlour off the main hall, visible the moment he stepped inside, and he recognised a few faces. One of them—a saucy redhead named Madeline—cast him a sunny grin and a wave.

"Fancy seeing you here, Mr Walker. Come to keep us company?"

He returned the grin with one of his own and removed the cap from his head. "As much fun as that would be, I was hoping to see Jasper."

The giggling girls fell silent, and Madeline's smile dimmed somewhat. The door opened behind Lucas, and another man stepped in and around him into the parlour, clearly a regular, and while the other girls all clamoured to greet him, Madeline stood and crossed over to Lucas, looping her arm through his and leading him back out into the hall.

"You really ought to go before Beatrice sees you here."

Lucas scowled, tugging his arm free and looking down at her. "What's that s'posed to mean? Is Jasper all right?"

"He's fine, yeah." Worrying at her bottom lip, she cast a cursory look at the stairs. "Just trust me, Lucas."

"It ain't like him to avoid me like this," he pressed urgently. "If somethin's happened…"

"Look…" Madeline floundered. The floorboards creaked overhead, and she winced, yanking open the front door. "I can't talk about it, or she'll have me head. Give it a few days. He'll show back up; you have my word."

"But—"

Lucas found himself crowded outside and the door shut in his face, his frustration lighting anew.

He returned to The Rusty Duck out of restlessness, buying himself a drink and slouching into a seat near the corner to down it. As he sat there and mulled over the conversation, plenty of scenarios ran through his mind. Jasper was sick. Jasper had got into trouble with his bawd. Jasper had been roughed up by a patron… That last one set Lucas's rage off and made him see red. It had happened once before, and the ensuing fight that broke out between that cull and Lucas had not been pretty.

But if Jasper wouldn't even see him, how was he supposed to help?

Sometime later, amidst his stewing thoughts, another glass clanged onto the table, and Daniel Barker slid into the seat across from him. Lucas inwardly sighed. He wasn't in the mood for company. In retrospect, coming to a place where he'd be surrounded by people hadn't been the best idea.

"Evenin', Barker."

"Mr Walker, fancy seein' you here."

"Shouldn't I be the one sayin' that? I'm here all the time."

Daniel shrugged. "Came to deliver a note for you, actually. They told me you weren't staying here anymore."

"Nah, got me a place a few blocks away." He took a long pull from his glass. "What's the note?"

"Glass was asking for you." Barker slid an envelope across the table. It was sealed, and this time the writing on it was Henry's, not Barker's.

Lucas slipped the envelope into his coat pocket. He didn't much feel like opening it right there in front of someone. "Any idea what he wants?"

"Your guess is as good as mine. Seems to have taken a shine to you, though." Barker raised an eyebrow.

Lucas's face warmed. "What's that mean?"

"Means exactly what I said, mate." Barker smiled thinly, and it was awkward, like he wasn't the sort to smile often. "It means Glass is all about helping others, but he's always been pretty quiet about his own wants and needs. He dives into his work, gives money to those less fortunate, but he's always got this sort of…barrier. Like he's sitting in his own little castle, keeping everything else out."

Lucas dropped his gaze to his glass. "What makes you think he's taken any kinda shine to me, then?"

The other man shrugged. "Ordinarily, I'm his middleman. I find people to work for him. Every person in Henry Glass's employ is like us, you know—even the women that work in his household. When he sends out orders to someone outside the house, it goes through me." He pointed at Lucas. "But he brought you in on his own, and he's now sending you messages directly. I have no idea what's in that letter, and he's never done that before. He's never kept me out of correspondence."

Lucas tried to tell himself the heat in his body was just from the alcohol, which might have been a more convincing argument if he'd had more than a drink or two. His fingers were itching to take the letter out and read it, but then he'd have felt obligated to share its contents with Barker. "Has he ever let anyone stay over before?"

Barker's eyebrows rose sharply. "Guess that depends on how you define 'stay over'."

"How many ways is there?"

"Did you fuck him?"

The bluntness of the question made Lucas wince a little. "No. I slept in the guest room. He didn't seem interested in more than that."

"Like I said, mate—castle walls to scale with that one." Barker rubbed the back of his neck and thought about it. "I stayed a few nights when we first met, but only 'cause I was at death's door. He took care of me, offered me work once I was on the mend. Never happened with any of the others, as far as I know."

That simple insight into Glass and Barker's relationship was rather eye-opening, wasn't it? No wonder Barker was so loyal and protective of Glass. "You'd consider yourself friends, then?"

"I'd like to think so, but I'm not always so sure." He laughed shortly, downed the remainder of his drink, and stood. "Rather hard to have friends when you keep everyone at arm's length, ain't it? If you see yourself in any kind of position to change that, I encourage it. Now if you'll excuse me, procuring bodies for Mr Glass is not the only work I do and I'm runnin' late."

He tipped his chin in a nod and made to leave. Before he could get far, Lucas found himself lurching to his feet to catch his arm as a sudden idea struck. "Hey, wait, maybe you can help me with somethin'."

TWELVE

At noon the following day, Lucas met with Daniel Barker outside The Rusty Duck. They walked to The Sun and Stars and paused at the end of the street, where Lucas handed over some money and a carefully written note.

Barker pocketed them and glanced down the road. "Jasper Rees, is it?"

"Yeah, but ask for Jasmine. They ain't gonna let in a stranger using his real name."

"Right. What am I askin' him, exactly?"

"Just give 'im that note, and make sure he's all right." Lucas wrung his hands together. "It ain't like him to be holed up in there like this."

"And why aren't you doing this yourself?"

"'Cause his bawd can't stand the sight of me. If she spots me or spots you 'n' me together, she won't let you in, neither."

Barker gave a curt nod and headed off down the street. Lucas sighed, slouching back against the storefront on the corner, and waited. Time slowed to a crawl there in the cold, where he watched the passers-by, and occasionally looked up at the sky. How long before the drizzle turned to a steady rain and, eventually, snow? It was an entirely reflexive feeling, being afraid of that. To say there were nights last winter when he almost didn't wake up after a night spent outside was not an exaggeration.

It was close to an hour before Barker returned. Lucas caught sight of him and pushed away from the building, heart in his throat, but the other man's expression gave nothing away.

Barker came to a halt, hands crammed deep into his pockets. "No worries. He's fine."

Some of the nervous tension in Lucas's chest vanished. "What's happened?"

Barker rolled his shoulders back. "I'm not supposed to tell you he took a good walloping from a cull."

Lucas's eyes narrowed. "*Who?* What happened??"

"He wouldn't tell me *that* much," Barker scoffed. "But he's in a spot of trouble with the procuress too, for the whole thing. Said the details were unimportant and that he ought to be back out and about in a week or so."

I'm gonna find out who it was and murder 'em, Lucas thought repeatedly. He'd drag it out of Jasper, or he'd bribe one of the girls to tell him if he had to.

He breathed in deep until the cold air made his lungs hurt. "You were in there a bit."

Barker snorted as they turned back down the road the way they'd come. "I didn't take advantage of the time I paid for, if that's what you're implying."

"Not your type?"

"Pretty little thing, to be sure, but no."

Lucas wondered if he ought to be defensive on Jasper's behalf at that. "What's your type, then?"

They fell into step, heading back in the direction of The Duck. Barker gazed off down the street, long lashes lowered and a reflective look upon his face. "That's a good question. I'd like to be able to answer it someday."

THIRTEEN

The note Barker had given him was an invitation to dinner.

A very proper invitation, at that: wax-sealed, formally addressed.

Mr Glass requests the pleasure of Mr Walker's company at dinner, Sunday, December 3rd, at seven o'clock. R.S.V.P.

Glass's address was underneath, as though Lucas didn't already know it, but it made him smile all the same. He wasn't honestly sure what R.S.V.P. stood for, but he knew what it meant, more or less. What he didn't know was the proper way to respond. Did he send a letter back? Did he hunt down Barker and ask him to deliver a message? Seemed a bit rude, asking him to play middle-man. Glass likely paid him for his time, and Lucas had already asked him for a favour in helping with Jasper.

In the end, he wrote on the back of the invitation: *Mr Walker would be happy to join Mr Glass for dinner.* He made it sound as proper as he knew how from hearing Henry himself speak, though his own poor scrawl diminished the effect he'd been going for.

When the next night arrived, he dressed in the clothes Glass had bought for him. Aside from his cap, which he was unwilling to leave behind, he might have almost passed for a proper gentleman.

Since it had begun to lightly snow the night before, he hailed a cab near The Duck to take him across town rather than going it on foot. This go around, he knew he'd arrive on time, maybe even a smidge early, and his nervousness was significantly tamer than at their first meal together. Having some idea of what to expect helped with that.

Frederick ushered him in. Hilda bounded down the hall, jumping at his legs until he stooped to pick her up and lavish some attention on her as he walked to the dining room. He was the first to arrive, though Glass entered shortly after he'd taken a seat.

Glass smiled in such a way that his eyes positively sparkled. "You're looking particularly dashing tonight."

Lucas had politely removed his cap upon entering the house, and now he reached up to touch his combed hair, feeling lost without the brim of the cap to mess with out of embarrassment.

"Thanks. Got the outfit compliments of this handsome gent who saw fit to bestow it upon me."

"I see your flattery is in full form tonight, as well."

They ate while alternating between companionable silence and light conversation. Lucas inquired about his work, something Glass apparently could talk about with ease and at length, relaying stories of various patients and peers. Glass inquired about Lucas's new lodgings—Lucas promised to write down the address before he departed that night, so future invitations could be sent to him directly.

Lucas found his gaze dropping to Glass's hands, watching as he cut into his roast, and he imagined him instead cutting into a person with that same practised care. It made him simultaneously queasy and amazed.

"I've been wonderin'… What made you decide to be a surgeon?"

Glass looked up. It was a far more personal question, asking about a man's background and upbringing, and Lucas had taken care not to tread into such topics before, but it just came out. If Glass was offended, however, that didn't show.

"My mother, actually," he said.

"She wanted you to be one?"

"Not at all. My father was a physician. Growing up, it was presumed I would follow in his footsteps. A beloved family practitioner, there to usher generations in and to see them comfortably to their last breath..."

"So, what changed?"

"Mother fell ill. A tumour took up residence in her body, and no amount of medicine or bed rest or blood-letting could help her. When Father's methods failed to improve her condition, there was a string of other doctors parading in and out of our home, looking her over, every one of them declaring she was beyond hope.

"They all said she would be dead before the end of the year, and we could only hope to make her comfortable. Mother was resigned to that prognosis, but Father refused to give up. He insisted she see a surgeon."

Lucas found himself putting down his cutlery, too interested in hearing this story to focus on his food. Worried, even, that perhaps he'd brought up a topic that might have negative memories for Mr Glass.

But Glass continued with a smile upon his face. "He laboured over her for hours. I was terrified, of course. I'd grown up being taught that surgery was only for the direst of circumstances, that it meant certain death in most cases. I was so *aghast* at the idea of someone cutting into her, removing things from her body."

"Did she... I mean, is she..."

"Oh, yes. Mother is quite well, still kicking around. No more than a scar and a limp that only really makes itself a nuisance when the weather is particularly poor."

A smile tugged at Lucas's mouth. "Made you wanna start doing it then?"

"Indeed. I announced my plans to my parents before Mother was even off bed rest. I was fascinated. I wanted to be like that man, capable of performing such miracles of medicine and science." A server slipped into the room, and Glass gave her a nod, letting her know she could clear his plate. "Since you asked about me, does that give me permission to ask about your family?"

Lucas crammed another bite of food into his mouth before allowing the woman to take his plate as well. "Nothin' so interesting as your story, really."

"No one's own story is particularly interesting to themselves, Mr Walker."

"Yeah, well…" He lowered his lashes, wondering what there really was to tell. "Mum died when I was five. Don't remember much about her. Dad… He went when I was twelve."

The good humour faded from Henry Glass's face. "You were so young."

He rolled his shoulders back into a shrug. "S'how it goes. People work themselves to death in the East End, you know. But it's fine. I made do. Caught rats for a couple of years for the city, 'til I got too big, then I started in with the factory work." He touched a hand to the cap in his lap. He'd politely refused to let Frederick take it when he'd arrived earlier. He had little to remember his parents by. No photographs, no sentimental hand-me-downs. Just the battered old hat his father had worn up until the day he died.

"I'm so sorry," Glass murmured, but Lucas flashed him a grin.

"To be honest, talkin' about them now and again feels kinda nice. They were good folks."

"They produced a son like you," Glass said with the gentlest of smiles, "so I can't imagine they were anything but good."

The two finished their meal in silence, and afterwards, they retired to the parlour for drinks and more conversation by the fire.

"You've everything you need at your new home?" Glass asked.

Lucas considered. He had everything he *needed*, really. There were certainly plenty of things he could have *used*, but nothing he couldn't—and hadn't for years—lived without. Extra blankets, more clothes. Besides that, he didn't want to give Glass any ideas that he needed anyone to buy him anything else. He wasn't there to take advantage of the man's generosity.

"Think my new job's helped me get situated well enough," was the answer he offered.

"I'm glad to hear it. Mr Barker said you appeared in good spirits. He seems quite fond of you, you know."

"Is that somethin' special?"

"He's a bit of a prickly man but a good judge of character, so, yes."

It made Lucas think about how highly Barker thought of Mr Glass, too. "Seems like a good enough bloke. We get on pretty well. He helped me out with a friend the other day."

Glass tipped his head. "Oh?"

Lucas looked down at his drink, uncertain how much he wanted to divulge. He did his best to avoid topics that highlighted how drastically different their lives were, topics that embarrassed him, but then he felt guilty for thinking that anything involving his friends ought to shame him. Jasper was easily the least embarrassing thing about his life.

"My friend, Jasper. He's—ah, he works in The…" He floundered. Was there really no elegant way to say *he's a whore*? "He works at a brothel."

Glass squinted, then his expression smoothed out. "Ah. Is that where you got the idea that you could do the same?"

His tone came across as playful, and it made Lucas's cheeks pinken. "Yeah, well… Anyway, he and I spend a lot of our free time together, and he went missin' for a few days. His bawd is a real piece of work and wouldn't tell me nothin', so Barker went in for me to make sure he was all right."

"And was he?"

Lucas paused. "After a fashion, I guess. Barker says he got roughed up by a customer."

That brought a frown to Glass's face. "That's horrible. I'm so sorry."

"S'happened before, but it ain't a regular occurrence." He shrugged, not wanting how much it bothered him to be overly apparent.

Silence loomed over the room for a moment before Glass asked, softly,

"Is he your lover, then?"

Lucas's gaze snapped over to meet his. It was a peculiar question, though maybe not altogether surprising. He and Jasper *did* spend a lot of time together; they were close—emotionally, physically—but that was all it had ever been.

Instead of saying *no* right away, Lucas found himself asking, "Rather bold question, ain't it?"

Glass shifted in his chair and tipped his head away, breaking eye contact. "Merely making conversation."

"Is it because you wanna know if I'm involved with someone? Because *you're* interested?"

"Now *that* is a bold question."

"Just makin' conversation."

Glass stared into the fire. He didn't respond.

But that lack of response in and of itself was an answer to Lucas. He set his drink aside, gaze unwavering from Glass's nervous, handsome face. Not for the first time, he tried to place the other man's age. Late thirties, perhaps. The beginnings of fine lines around his eyes and mouth, a bit of grey in his hair. Potentially early forties, even—and the difference in age might have bothered some men like Lucas, barely into his twenties, but he wasn't most men.

When he looked at Henry Glass, he saw a man with a kind heart and an empathy many lacked. He saw someone who strived to make the world a better place in whatever little ways he could.

He also saw a man who was very lonely.

Lucas rose from his chair, almost involuntarily, the troubled look on Glass's face drawing Lucas across the distance separating them. He lifted a hand and brought his fingers to the freshly shaved curve of Glass's jaw, a gentle touch that prompted the other man to look up at him.

"Jasper and I are just friends," he said softly. "Nothin' else."

A flicker of something resembling hope brewed with uncertainty shone in the hazel depths of his eyes. "A shame for him."

Lucas almost laughed. "Not so much for you, though, yeah?"

Then he braced his other hand on the back of Henry Glass's chair, leaned down, and kissed him.

Was it the right thing to do? He had no idea. But it seemed the *only* thing to do when Glass was looking at him like that, begging to be kissed but too afraid to ask for it. Much to Lucas's pleasure, the other man's breath hitched, and his lips parted, and he tipped his head to better fit their mouths together, turning what Lucas intended to be soft and chaste into something much more.

He slid his fingers from Glass's jaw to the back of his neck, holding him in place, and sank down into his lap while Glass's arms slowly went around his middle. Everything Glass did was so careful and cautious. Lucas thought about what Barker had said—all those castle walls. He would have given anything to see into Glass's head just then, to understand what he was thinking, how he was feeling, what it was that made him so reluctant to let himself enjoy the moment completely.

Because *he* was enjoying it. Glass's mouth tasted of the wine he'd had at dinner and had continued to partake of there in the parlour, something a bit sweet. The hands against Lucas's back, fisting into the fabric of his shirt, were so warm, and he ached to know what they would feel like against his skin.

And when he moved just so in Glass's lap, he could feel the man—hard and most definitely interested—and the sensation had Lucas letting out a heady groan into the kiss.

Then Glass pulled away.

He didn't immediately break all contact with Lucas, no, but he drew back from the kiss and sucked in a breath as if a spell had been broken, although his eyes were still glazed over with want. But they weren't kissing anymore, and Lucas couldn't for the life of him understand *why*.

Then Glass uncurled his fingers from Lucas's shirt and returned them to the arms of the chair. "I think…"

Carefully controlled emotions. Walls up. *Barriers.*

"…We ought to call it a night."

Even his voice was thick and low and rippled down Lucas's spine. Damn him. It was a stark contrast to the words leaving his lips.

Lucas tried to tamp down the overwhelming sense of rejection coupled with guilt and shame. "Did I do somethin' wrong?"

"No, no, dear boy." Glass lifted a hand, like he might touch Lucas's cheek, but lowered it again before he did. "This is simply—I'm sorry. It might just be better…"

He'd been turned down before. Of course he had. What man hadn't been? But the fact that he *knew* Henry Glass wanted him and was turning him away regardless left Lucas reeling in confusion and frustration. Did it have to do with his status? His upbringing, his age? Had he said or done something wrong during dinner?

Fine.

Lucas slid to his feet. The sudden lack of physical contact made every inch of his soul ache. He snatched his cap from beside his chair.

"Lucas," Glass started to say, and the sound made Lucas flinch.

"Thank you kindly for dinner, Mr Glass," he said coolly, tugging the cap onto his head. "I should be heading home."

He left before Glass could stop him.

Two could play at this game. He had his own walls to fortify.

FOURTEEN

What in the hell were you thinking, you bloody fool? Henry asked himself again and again. How had he let the situation get as far as it had? It certainly hadn't been his intention when he'd invited Lucas over for dinner.

No, that was not entirely true.

Although Henry might not always have been the most honest about his intentions and feelings with others, he tried so hard to maintain honesty with himself. Which meant fully acknowledging what had happened and accepting responsibility for it; he was hardly innocent. Perhaps he'd not *consciously* encouraged any of this, but the fact remained that some part of him had not minded Lucas Walker kissing him.

And a part of him had desperately wanted it.

Henry was painfully aware of his blossoming feelings…a blend of attraction and fascination and adoration. Lucas was young, yes. But he'd faced more in his young life than had many men Henry's own age. He was kind-hearted and persistent, and those brilliant, sunny smiles of his made Henry's heart soar in a way he'd not felt in *years*.

Which only made him more the fool, he felt. What good could possibly come from this? These sorts of things led to heartbreak, sorrow, and loneliness. No matter how much one wanted, no matter how much one hoped and prayed…

He knew from experience.

Once upon a time, he'd loved a man and then lost him. He did not think he could go through that again.

The scene from the other night rattling about in his head made focusing on work difficult. He did his best to abandon his personal struggles at the door each morning he entered St. Mary's Hospital, knowing he had men and women and children relying on him to maintain his composure, to have his full attention upon the task at hand—or the body on the table, as it were.

It was with steady hands and an equally steady voice, speaking to the auditorium of students and fellow surgeons, that Henry tended to that day's patient. A young man with an abnormal growth on his neck, something too close to too many vital veins and arteries so that most surgeons refused to operate on him, but Henry had taken up the mantle. He explained to his enrapt audience each step he made, the precautions he took, and spoke of prior experiences in the removal of malignant masses from his patients. More often than not, they had made a full recovery. Sometimes, the tumours came back. Sometimes they stayed gone for good.

"The important thing to note," Henry said, "is that the use of medical science and surgery bought them time and quality of life they'd otherwise have lost."

At some point during his operation, Henry took note of a familiar face in the crowd and glanced up, squinting. Daniel Barker looked out of place there, hands in his pockets, not taking notes like the rest of the class. Certainly not as well-dressed as most of them.

It wouldn't be until the room had cleared and his patient had been wheeled away to recovery that Henry could even acknowledge him. He gave Daniel a nod, turned, and proceeded out the opposite door, leading him to the offices in the back of the hospital.

Away from the bright gas lamps of the stuffy auditorium, Henry sighed, peeling off his apron and dabbing a towel across his forehead. Daniel dropped into a chair nearby.

"Always fascinating to see you work."

"Is it? I fret about being a bore."

"Not in the least."

Henry turned to give him a small smile. "Thank you. Is everything well?"

Daniel shrugged. "Yeah, fine. Just thought I'd come to give you this, see if you were interested."

He slipped a piece of paper from his pocket and offered it out for Henry to take. When Henry opened it, he read the name, age, sex, and cause of death of a man recently deceased. Another mass, this one not even noticed until after death when the family had been convinced foul play was involved and an autopsy had been performed. Interesting.

"He's being interred in the mornin'," Daniel said. "So, if you want him, we'd need to snatch him tomorrow night."

Ordinarily, Henry would have had questions. Where Daniel came across this information, for instance. Not because he didn't trust Daniel implicitly, but out of pure curiosity.

This time, he only nodded. "Yes, that would be good."

Daniel paused and tipped his head. "Somethin' the matter?"

Henry turned to the nearby sink to pour himself a glass of water. "Hm? I'm quite all right. Probably tired. I've been busy as of late."

He couldn't see Daniel, but he could hear him. "Hm." Just a single sound, yet it managed to come across accusatory and disbelieving.

"What?"

"If you don't wanna discuss it, that's one thing, but I've known you long enough to be aware of the difference between you being 'distracted' and you being bothered by something."

Henry let out a breath and turned back around. "It's nothing, Daniel, honestly."

The other man pursed his lips, scrutinising as Henry easily downed half his glass while wishing it were something stronger. "Well, far be it from me to go digging into my employer's personal matters."

It was a subtle jab, but Henry felt it immensely, and it coaxed a sigh from his lips. "Don't be like that. I consider you someone to confide in, just... Oh, I don't know. I don't enjoy whinging."

Daniel scoffed. "You're not a man who *whinges*, Henry Glass. Whinging would imply you had no reason to complain about something."

His shoulders sagged the slightest bit. "I rarely feel I have cause to complain."

"Why don't you tell me about it, and I'll tell you if I think you're out of line or not."

"I'm certain you have better things to do than to listen to some old fool, but I appreciate your kindness."

He hoped that would be it because Daniel Barker was not a man to push and pry where he wasn't wanted...even though a part of Henry very much did want to speak to someone. To what end, he didn't know, just that the emotions felt coiled so tight in his chest that he feared they would burst free unbidden at any moment.

So, when all Daniel did was stare, intense blue eyes locked on him, knowing and patient, Henry's resolve began to crumble.

What he wouldn't give for a proper drink.

"I fear I may have made a mess of things with Mr Walker."

"Oh?"

How did he explain the situation vaguely enough to satisfy Daniel without giving too much away? "I meant to cultivate a friendship with him, and I think I may have subconsciously encouraged more."

Daniel's eyebrows raised. "What happened?"

Henry paused. "He kissed me."

If Daniel was the slightest bit surprised, it didn't show. "You kissed him back."

Not a question, but an observation. Was Henry truly so transparent? He grimaced but didn't try to deny it.

"All right, so…" Daniel slouched in his chair, arms crossed, so tall that he never quite seemed to fit in the spaces he tried to occupy. "He kissed you; you kissed him back. Two men kissing one another 'cause they wanted to. And there's a problem with this because…?"

Henry frowned. "There are a million problems with it. The only one of which ultimately matters is that I am not comfortable with it."

"Why? Is it his age?"

"I would consider that a contributing factor, yes, but not the only one."

Daniel rolled his eyes ceilingward. "Permission to speak out of line, Henry? As your friend, not your worker?"

Oh, Lord, he wanted to say no. It would be easier. Certainly, less of a headache. "Of course."

Daniel said, "You're an idiot."

Not what he'd expected. "Pardon?"

"You heard me. In the two years that I've known you, Henry Glass, I can count on one hand the number of times I've seen you go out of your way to try to get to know anyone. You aren't the sort to fuck and leave, and that's fine, but I know you're lonely. Now, some nice-looking lad crosses your path and shows interest in you, and you refuse to indulge yourself a bit? I swear, sometimes I think you don't *want* to be happy."

Ah, yes, there it was. The oncoming headache. He closed his eyes and breathed deep through his nose. "I'm really not interested in a lecture."

"Yeah, well. Sometimes we need to listen to things we don't want to hear." Daniel rose to his feet. "Ignore it if you want, but I'm right. You're a good man, and I won't pretend to understand the sheer amount of self-loathing you seem to cart around, but you should have a look at it sometime."

Self-loathing? Henry bristled, unable to help the slight surge of defensiveness he felt at those accusations. "A step too far, Mr Barker."

Daniel paused, jaw tense, and crammed his hands into his pockets. The sudden distant expression that passed over his features jabbed guilt between Henry's ribs. He reminded himself sharply that Daniel said these things out of a place of concern, not out of malice.

"Right. Well, I should be going," Daniel said.

"Daniel…"

"It's fine." He took a step back when Henry reached to touch his arm. "I crossed a line, but I won't apologise for speaking the truth. See you tomorrow night."

As he proceeded to leave, Henry dragged in a slow breath. "*Daniel.*"

The other man stopped and glanced back.

Henry managed a feeble smile. "Thank you."

Some of that tension eased out of Daniel's posture, his expression softening around his eyes, and he nodded once. "Things will get better, Henry. But only if you let them."

FIFTEEN

Barker sent for Lucas the following Thursday. Instead of the cemetery, the trio converged outside a pub several miles away. Lucas was grateful for that, and this time, he came better prepared. He wore two layers of socks, fingerless gloves, a scarf, and a wool coat. Items purchased second-hand, which would no doubt make a good work investment all the same.

They grabbed a drink at the pub along with a small supper to tide them over, and only then did they pile into the wagon and head off to a different cemetery than they'd gone to before.

This time, Lucas knew what to expect. And maybe his outing with Barker the previous week left him more comfortable overall, having come to view him as just another man who was not all that different from himself. Barker cared about Mr Glass, came from a background not unlike Lucas's, and he'd been a kind enough person to help Lucas with the Jasper situation while asking for nothing in return.

Pendleton was another case altogether. Something in the man's frigid demeanour did not sit well with Lucas, and he did his best to shrug it off. Lucas was, by all accounts, a replacement for the Barnaby kid that the group had lost. Maybe there was a story he wasn't privy to yet. Maybe Pendleton was just a prick.

Their target that night was another corpse who'd died after refusing an operation. It was a subject of interest to Glass, Barker explained as they dug into the fresh grave. After having heard Glass's story about his mum, Lucas could wager a guess why the subject of tumours fascinated him so much.

They retrieved the corpse, and Lucas didn't baulk this time, although the man had been dead longer than the last one and the smell nearly made him lose his supper. On the drive to Glass's house, Pendleton manned the horse, and Barker again slumped down in the back of the wagon with Lucas. They sat in tired, companionable silence, interrupted only by Barker asking, "Were you able to see your friend yet?"

To which Lucas sighed and shook his head. Barker offered a sympathetic look and a drink from his flask.

Lucas didn't want to say it wasn't Jasper who had his spirits down that night. Or that he'd put thought into cancelling on this job, or at the very least, not going with them for the drop-off. Seeing Glass again so soon after their dinner made his chest hurt and his stomach knot up.

I ain't gonna miss out on my money just 'cause he wants to be difficult, he told himself. He would not be chased away from employment. Maybe this was his own fault, at any rate. He should have known better than to kiss his employer.

At Glass's back door, they brought the dead man in and unloaded him onto the autopsy table. Lucas cast a look around, wondering just what Glass did with the bodies when he was finished with them. He didn't see any new additions to his jars on the shelves.

"No problems?" Glass asked of Barker as he doled out their payment.

"Not this time," Barker replied, and the two of them stared at each other, as though having some kind of conversation that Lucas and Pendleton weren't privy to. It stirred a bit of jealousy in Lucas's insides.

"What's all that, then? What's going on?" Pendleton asked with a scowl, seeming to pick up on the same thing.

Glass only gave a nod and turned away. Barker sighed. "I deliver bodies to a few other surgeons in the area, and security at some of the cemeteries has been increasing. I've had three jobs I've had to abandon because we almost got caught."

Pendleton's shoulders squared. "Wait—you been goin' on jobs without us?"

Barker levelled a patient look in his direction. "For other clients, yes. I go where I'm needed."

The redhead scowled. "Ain't that nice to know."

Lucas was hardly surprised; Barker had mentioned as much to him before. What he didn't get was why it mattered. "What's it to us if he's got more sources of income? Don't hurt us none."

Pendleton levelled that dark look at Lucas, grunted, and then headed for the door.

Barker rolled his eyes, and although he didn't say anything on the matter, he clapped Lucas briefly on the shoulder. "We ought to be going. Need a ride back?"

Lucas glanced at Mr Glass, aching to say no, that he'd stay here a bit longer. Maybe even overnight.

But, after their last time alone together, it didn't surprise Lucas in the least when Glass only smiled and averted his gaze as he said, "Please do, Mr Barker. No sense in having him walk home in the cold at this hour."

For as expected as it was, it still stung.

"'Night, *Mister* Glass," he said, clenching his jaw and heading out the door after Pendleton.

He nursed the empty feeling in his chest as they rode in silence, but the tension between Pendleton and Barker was palpable. There was something he couldn't place, but if Barker was bothered by the other's displeasure, it didn't show.

They dropped Lucas off near his place, and he contemplated going to The Sun and Stars in another attempt to see Jasper. Sleep seemed too daunting a task. But he also wasn't up for more rejection if Jasper wouldn't see him, so home it was, where he stripped down and fell into bed with a sigh.

He must have been more tired than he thought because the next thing he knew, someone was knocking on his door and light was streaming through the window right into his eyes. Groaning, he rolled out of bed. He really needed curtains.

"Hold a sec!"

He dragged on a fresh pair of drawers and his trousers, shuffled to the door and pulled it open.

On the other side stood Jasper, hair twisted back into a bun, a paper bag in hand. He smiled brightly. "Mornin'."

Lucas threw the door open and gathered his friend into a tight hug. "Christ almighty! You have any idea how fuckin' worried I've been?"

Jasper gave a breathless laugh and hugged him back, ruffling his hair. Lucas drew away, stepping aside to beckon him in.

"I'm so sorry, Lu. Tried getting a letter out to you, but none of the girls was willing to risk Beatrice's wrath if we got found out."

That was logical enough. Though it seemed unfair. Jasper was an incredible artist, but he also wrote and read better than most people Lucas knew. He'd taught several of the women at The Sun and Stars too—including basic mathematics. He insisted they all learn that much. Otherwise clients would swindle them on payments all the time.

"How'd you find this place on your own?" he asked.

Jasper held up a slip of paper with Lucas's address written in Barker's handwriting. "A few people were kind enough to point me in the right direction."

Lucas shut the front door and took the bag Jasper offered. Inside were two sizable *gateau* pastries. His mouth watered at the sight. They had a seat at the small table near the window, splitting the pastries between them.

Jasper was uncharacteristically quiet, though; he didn't ask Lucas about his place, about Barker, about how he'd managed to afford all this. The sunlight washing in through the dirty glass illuminated Jasper's warm skin enough that Lucas could make out the fading, mottled bruises along the side of his face. Anger roiled in his chest.

"You gonna tell me what happened?"

His friend exhaled in a way that suggested he'd been waiting for the question. He delicately licked the sugar and cream from his fingertips. "What do you think happened?"

"I'm thinkin' one of your culls got too rough. But I want details—like his damned name."

"It wasn't one of *my* patrons," Jasper gently corrected. "It was one of Madeline's. Ruby and I heard her screaming. We were the closest, so we kicked in the door and dragged him off her."

"Y'just had to play hero, huh?"

Jasper frowned. "He had his hands around her throat, Lu. He could have killed her."

Lucas's jaw clenched. "He coulda killed you instead."

"Maybe, but I wasn't going to sit by and do nothing. You wouldn't have, either."

Their eyes met, and Jasper lifted his chin defiantly, daring Lucas to say what was on his mind. *I'm stronger than you are. You're too delicate; you're too gentle.* It wasn't a fair judgement, and Lucas knew that, so he bit it back. But it was true. Jasper was gentle and soft and didn't have a violent bone in his body.

Lucas broke eye contact and tucked another piece of pastry into his mouth. "So, what happened then? You handle him?"

"Between Ruby and me, we got him outside, and some gents from down the way were kind enough to step in."

Not before the bloke got in a few good hits, it looked like. "Not gonna tell me his name, I wager."

Jasper's smile turned a bit tight. "Not unless you promise not to go after him."

It wasn't likely, running into one single stranger in a sea of them—but it was possible. The last time had been at The Rusty Duck, and the moment a customer had got too handsy with Jasper had been the moment Lucas put the man's head through a window.

To be fair, he'd insisted later, *if I hadn't of done it, someone else would've.* Because Jasper's face was one many of the regulars at The Duck knew and loved.

"I can't promise that, and you know it."

"Then I'm not going to tell you." Jasper snagged another piece of pastry to pop it into his mouth, then swept his hand about the flat. "So, it's your turn now."

Lucas shrugged. "Told you, got me some new employment. Look, I even got meself a bed to sleep in."

"Hm."

"What's that for?"

"For you being intentionally evasive about this job. What are you doing?"

"Stuff," he replied lamely.

"Hm," again. He hated that sound.

"Remember that night I went over to Mr Glass's? He offered me some work."

Jasper studied him, waiting.

He wanted to lie, but Jasper would find out the truth eventually, and then he'd be hurt, and that would be a disaster. Hurting Jasper was like kicking a damned baby.

Sighing, Lucas abandoned his food and slouched gracelessly back into his seat. "Right, right. Look, you're gonna be mad…"

"Do I get mad?"

"You get *quiet.* Which is kinda like your version of angry and, honestly, it's worse."

Jasper crossed his arms. Continued waiting. Patiently.

"Mr Glass is a surgeon, like I said. He does research on his own time, and research like that requires—well…"

Did he need to spell it out further? Jasper wasn't stupid.

Sure enough, his friend frowned first, and then his dark eyes grew wide in horror. "*Lucas.*"

He hunkered down further in his chair, chastened. "A-yep."

"You're *body-snatching?*"

"I mean, I guess I've heard it called that…"

Jasper shoved back his chair, rose to his feet, and began to pace the short span of the room. Quietly. As Lucas knew he would. Finally, he swivelled, sat on the edge of the bed, and stared at Lucas with his brows knitted together in concern. "All right. All right." Softly, trying to keep himself calm, not that the situation was all right but that *he* needed to be all right because that was the sort of man Jasper was.

Lucas took in a slow, deep breath. "I'm sorry I didn't say nothin' sooner. I didn't want you to worry."

Jasper shook his head and closed his eyes, lifting his fingers to press against his temples. "I feel like listing all the reasons this is a horrible idea would be lost on you."

"As lost as it is on you when I've tried talkin' you out of your line of work."

"That's different."

"How? What you do is dangerous too. I ain't walked away after being beaten by a cull."

Jasper's cheeks coloured, but he had no retort for that.

"And," Lucas continued, dredging up the same argument Glass had used on him, "it ain't *technically* illegal to take bodies so long as I ain't stealin' anything they was buried with."

Jasper huffed. However, instead of arguing, he deflated a little and folded his hands in his lap. Lucas took the silence to mean he was winning. Except 'winning' against Jasper never really felt like much of a victory. Lucas stood and crossed the room, taking a seat beside Jasper and leaning into him.

"Look, I *need* this job. You know I do. I'm being careful, and the lads I'm workin' with know what they're doing, yeah?" He gave Jasper's shoulder a gentle nudge with his own. "I got my own place for the first time in over a year. I got food on the table. Hell, you know you could come stay here with me now."

Jasper jerked his head slightly, side-eyeing him. "What?"

Lucas held up a hand. "Hear me out. You ain't fond of that old bawd. So, keep doin' your work, if it pleases you. But come live *here*."

For half a moment, Jasper almost seemed to consider it. His gaze swept the room. It wasn't much, Lucas knew, but it was more than Jasper had at The Sun and Stars. It was more than he'd have if he tried to live on his own.

But even before Jasper opened his mouth, Lucas knew what the answer was going to be.

"I appreciate the offer…"

"But…no?" He let out a frustrated sigh. "Why in the hell not?"

Jasper shook his head. "Just like you never wanted to take me up on my offer to sneak in and stay with me at night, even when the alternative meant sleeping in the cold, just like you refused to ever seek help from the workhouses… I never asked why you made the decisions that you did, and I need you to understand and respect my choices now."

When presented with an argument like that, it would have made him a complete arse to protest, wouldn't it? Lucas opened his mouth, wishing he could just grab Jasper and shake some sense into him. It wasn't Lucas taking care of him; it was them taking care of each other. They were best friends, like brothers, and what good was Lucas if he couldn't even help the man seek a better life?

He looked down at his hands on his knees and exhaled heavily through his nose. "Yeah, all right."

"Thanks, Lu. Now, I have to get back." Jasper pressed his palm briefly to

Lucas's cheek as he stood. After fetching his coat and starting for the door, he paused to cast a look over his shoulder. "I'm really happy for you, you know. I just worry."

Lucas forced a smile. "I know. Me too."

SIXTEEN

Work remained steady. Throughout the month of November, as the weather went from chilled but bearable to freezing, Lucas piled into the wagon with Barker and Pendleton and delivered bodies to Mr Glass. During that time, Lucas squirrelled away whatever money he could, cautioned by Barker that, once summer hit, work would slow because it was harder to find fresh bodies before the heat got to them.

Barker also, after dropping off Pendleton first after a job one night, asked Lucas if he wanted in on more work.

Lucas startled. "For your other employers, you mean?"

Barker shrugged. "Got room for another set of hands, is all. Don't feel obligated."

He chewed at his lip. More money was always good. Glass paid well, but it wasn't like Lucas was living in luxury or anything. "Why me? Why not Pendleton?"

"Why would it need to be Pendleton?"

"Dunno. You two have been workin' together awhile, haven't you?"

"Yeah, but we don't get on that great, and he threw a fit when he found out I wasn't letting him in on this to begin with. Got no room in my life for petulant children."

Things had seemed a little tense between the pair since that revelation. If

Pendleton found out Lucas was in on the other work too, would it make matters worse?

But money was money, so, after a moment— "Yeah, all right. If you need me."

Barker came for him three days later with two men Lucas didn't know. He doubted they were of the same sort he, Barker, and Pendleton were, and they came across as gruff and unapproachable, more the types of people Lucas would have imagined would be resurrectionists. He didn't speak to them overmuch, preferring to keep close to Barker's side as though his companion's shadow would make him invisible.

They went on three raids over the next week, and although the buyers weren't nearly so gracious with their money as Glass, it was still something for Lucas to save away. On the second week, when Barker pulled up to the appointed cemetery, they paused, noting immediately the wagon that was parked just outside the front gates.

"Someone's beaten us here," said Deacon, a burly middle-aged man with thinning hair.

"Could've been put there as a means of scarin' us off," said Fitch, the other man, who spoke with a thick Welsh accent.

Barker let out a long breath that puffed in front of his face in the cold. "Not likely. Told you, security has been gettin' tight."

"So, now what?" Fitch growled.

"We come back another night."

"Are you fuckin' kidding me?" Deacon slammed his shovel down into the back of the wagon. "I got rent to pay and a family to feed, Barker. You ought to be staking these places out better!"

Lucas glanced at Barker, whose face remained a blank slate. He'd seemed off-kilter all night, slower to respond, as though walking in a fog, but his steadfastness, his inability to be flustered even when things did not go as planned, was a character trait Lucas had come to admire. "I said what I said, mate. We're not going in."

"Fuck that." Fitch hopped from the wagon and grabbed his shovel. "Let's go. If we dig up that body an' bring it back all by ourselves, you ain't gettin' a cut of the payment."

Lucas and Barker exchanged a look. They could get out of there, Lucas knew, but doing so would mean leaving Fitch and Deacon to fend for themselves and, if that happened, their working relationship was done for. Or they could wait and let the other men do the dangerous work and forego any money to be made. Lucas could see Barker running the options through his head before he swore under his breath, grabbed a lantern, and hopped out of the wagon to follow the others.

Lucas scurried after him. "You sure about this?"

"Not at all," Barker muttered. "You see anyone else, drop what you're doing and run. Got it?"

Lucas responded with a tight nod. He didn't need to be told twice. *Technical* legality notwithstanding, law enforcement would haul them in and try to pin them with something, even if it were something made up. Lucas didn't see fit to spend any time behind bars.

They crept through the skeletal trees and snow as quietly as they were able. Barker dimmed the flame of his lamp as much as he could without extinguishing it, relying on moonlight to guide their way. Most of the graves sat blanketed in sheets of snow, so their fresh grave stood out like a sharp bruise upon the earth. They halted around the site, turning every which way, watching, listening, for any signs that they were not alone.

Fitch turned and thrust a shovel into Lucas's hands. "Get to work."

They dug as swiftly and efficiently as they could, switching off as necessary. The others would keep watch, jumping at every sound.

"My granny could dig faster than you, Barker," Deacon hissed at one point. And as much as Lucas hated to admit it, Barker *was* moving uncharacteristically slow.

Barker paused, leaning against his shovel, hands gripping the handle tight. When he lifted one to wipe the sweat from his brow, Lucas noticed he was trembling.

Although still recovering from his last turn, Lucas slipped down into the sizable hole, reaching for the shovel as he gently said, "Go on, I got this."

Barker cast him a guilty but grateful look and crawled out to leave him to it.

Despite the cold, soon Lucas was sweating, and his muscles burned with the exertion. He'd told himself this would get easier, but every job proved just as exhausting as the last. Especially now, with the fear of discovery looming over his head and the weather pitted against them. He worked as quickly as he could, though his body protested every second of it. The sooner they got this done, the sooner they could get the hell out of there.

"Barker, the hell's wrong with you?" Fitch called into the darkness.

Lucas stole a look up and over the edge of the grave. Barker had meandered away from them a few feet, staring into the shadows with his head tipped. Motionless, unresponsive. At first, Lucas thought maybe his friend had spotted something, but as the seconds ticked by, it became apparent something was off.

He stopped digging, brow furrowed. "Barker? You all right?"

The lantern slipped from Barker's hand, going out when it struck the snow.

A second later Daniel, too, crumpled to the ground.

Deacon swore. Lucas launched himself out of the grave, throwing the shovel to Deacon and bolting over to Barker's side.

Barker's eyes had rolled back, and his spine had gone rigid, hands fisted tight against his chest as though lightning were shocking every nerve in his body. Lucas had seen people have fits before, just a handful of times, so he recognised it for what it was—but that didn't mean he had any damned idea about what to do to help.

"Barker, Barker, hey…" he murmured, dropping to his knees and coaxing his friend onto his side. A look over at Deacon and Fitch revealed neither of them gave a good damn what was going on because they were still digging like mad, not so much as asking if Barker was all right.

All Lucas could do was keep a hand on Barker's shoulder, holding him on his side, watching helplessly as his limbs quivered like a puppet fighting against its too-tight strings. The next minute slowed into what felt like hours. Finally, Barker's body began to go limp and, Lord, his face was so blue, or maybe that was the moonlight; Lucas didn't know, but it was scaring him, and *what the hell was he supposed to do?*

Then Barker dragged in a quaking breath as though emerging from water, like his lungs were starved for it, and Lucas cried out in relief.

"Easy, mate," he crooned, drawing the other's head into his lap instead of having him lie on the hard, cold ground. Barker's hands uncurled, curled again, flexing, and he rolled his eyes up to Lucas, blinking slowly but not speaking.

He heard Fitch let out a triumphant *whoop*, signifying they'd reached the body, and Lucas glared in their direction.

Deacon and Fitch loaded the corpse into the sack and made quick work of filling the grave back up again. By that point, Barker had begun to try to move away, but he was still shaky and still not speaking.

"Get a move on," Deacon snapped at them. "Or we're takin' the wagon and leavin' your sorry arses behind."

Lucas bit his tongue to fend off a furious retort. Maybe they weren't *friends* with Barker, but they worked with the man often enough. Didn't that call for some level of concern for his well-being?

He looked down at Barker, who had managed to prop himself up on one elbow and was trying to sit up on his own. Snow flecked his curly hair and eyelashes, had soaked into his clothes just as it had through the knees of Lucas's trousers.

Lucas crawled to his feet and leaned down to help the man up. "C'mon, s'all right. Lean on me if you need to."

Barker mumbled something under his breath that might have been a *thank you*. He wobbled once upright, likely disoriented, and permitted Lucas to put an arm around his middle and help him along after the others.

Outside the cemetery, Fitch and Deacon loaded the body into its crate and swung up into the driver's bench while Lucas dragged Barker into the back of the wagon. They rode in frigid silence. Still, neither of the men turned around to ask after Barker, who lay down and instantly fell asleep beside him. Lucas kept checking to make sure he was still breathing.

They reached their buyer's home, unloaded the wagon, and took their payment. Lucas squinted as Fitch counted out the coins.

"Where's Barker's piece?"

"He don't get one," Deacon scoffed. "We all did most o' the work."

Anger flared hotly under Lucas's skin. "Nah, mate. Barker did the research on the body, it was his wagon that transported us, and he did some of the diggin'."

Fitch turned to him, eyes narrowed. "Fuck off, boy. Give 'im some of your share if you're so chummy."

Both men towered over him by a good half a foot, at least. Outweighed him, too. But Lucas stood firm, mouth drawn tight.

"Hand over his cut of the pay, or I'll be makin' sure the lot of you don't get a cut of *nothin'* in this business ever again." It was a barefaced lie. Certainly not a threat he could back up, but it was worth a try.

Deacon paused, huffed, then turned away. "Give 'im the damn money, Fitch."

Lucas held out his hand. Glaring murderously, Fitch crammed both Barker's payment and Lucas's own into his outstretched fingers. He counted to make sure it was all there, then gave a tight smile and a tip of his cap. "Pleasure doin' business with you."

He swung up into the driver's bench and gathered the reins. When

Deacon and Fitch went to get on, Lucas snapped the reins and the horses jolted forward a few paces.

"The fuck?" Fitch snarled.

"Nice night out," Lucas said coolly. "Have a lovely evening, gentlemen."

With that, he gave the reins another flick and then started forward, trotting off down the cobblestone road.

Let the pricks walk home, he thought bitterly.

A few blocks away, he stole a look back into the wagon where Barker was still out cold. What did he do now? He didn't know where Barker lived, didn't know where to take him, and he couldn't very well go back to his place—the wagon and horse would likely be stolen in the night. Besides, if Barker was unwell, then he needed...

He needs a doctor.

SEVENTEEN

The packages had arrived barely a week after Henry had ordered them, and he'd placed them atop his dresser where they'd remained for the last two months. One night, he'd unfolded each article and looked it over, admiring the careful stitching and the crisp, new fabric. Picturing how all of it would look on Lucas was easy…except that from the very day he'd ordered it, he hadn't been so certain he ought to give the clothing after all. What he'd intended to be a simple act of friendship and kindness had clearly been a step too far, if Lucas's reaction had been an indicator. Henry should have known right then that he was getting in over his head.

November had passed by in a blur of miserable, rainy weather and brief exchanges with Lucas. Always polite, but always curt, to the point, both avoiding any time alone together. Lucas arrived with Daniel and left with Daniel, and if words did not need to be exchanged between Lucas and Henry, then they refrained from doing so.

Henry hated it with every fibre of his being.

Self-loathing, Daniel had said to him. He'd been insulted by such a remark at the time. Later, as he'd lain in bed and drifted off to sleep, recalling Lucas's mouth, the taste of Lucas's tongue against his; as he'd slipped a hand beneath the bedding, wrapped his fingers about his cock and brought himself to a messy and largely unsatisfying release, and proceeded to be disgusted with himself…

He'd come to the conclusion that Daniel was not that far off.

As he reflected on all of this, not for the first time, the sound of someone pounding on a door somewhere made him pause mid-drink. He lifted his head, listened, until the sound came again. The cellar door, wasn't it?

With a frown, Henry set aside his glass, nudged Hilda out of his lap, and hurried through the house, spurred on by the urgency in that repeated, frantic knocking. Nearly two in the morning, when he did not expect any deliveries from Daniel and the others—who in the world would be at his back doorstep?

He opened the door mid-knock, greeted promptly by a wide-eyed, distressed face.

"Lucas?"

"It's Barker," Lucas all but cried, gesturing to the wagon in the alley behind him. "We were on a job, and he just…he just collapsed. I don't know what happened, he…"

Dread rose wild and fierce in Glass's chest, and he tamped it down, refusing to allow Lucas's panic to infect him. He pulled the door open all the way, bringing a hand to Lucas's shoulder. "Easy."

Just like that, Lucas's shoulders slumped, somewhere between tired and relieved.

Henry stepped outside, ignoring the cold that burned into the soles of his bare feet and slithered its way up beneath his nightclothes and dressing gown. Daniel lay in the back of his wagon, quiet and still. Henry didn't even need to ask what had happened.

"Come along, let's get him inside."

Daniel was not easily roused. He opened his eyes when Lucas and Henry prodded at him but was largely unresponsive to any of Henry's questions. Still, he shuffled through the cellar with Lucas on one side and Henry on the other while towering over them both.

They helped him stumble his way upstairs and into the spare room. Henry waved Lucas back, set about ridding Daniel of his damp coat and shirt, and sat at his bedside. He looked over the man, lifting his eyelids, checking his pulse, all while Lucas lingered near the door with his cap wrung tightly in his hands.

It had been some time since Henry had seen Daniel in such a state. *Not long enough,* he thought dismally. Still, pulse was steady, breathing sounded fine. Daniel was simply worn out.

"Is he gonna be all right?" Lucas asked.

Henry drew the blankets up around Daniel, then rose and ushered Lucas back into the hall to let their companion rest in peace. "He's going to be fine. This is the first time you've seen this?"

"From him? Well, yeah. Has it happened before?"

More times than you'd believe. Henry knew his own smile to be a sad one. "Let's get you something to drink."

Lucas frowned, not budging. "I ain't thirsty. What's goin' on?"

"It's hardly my place to tell you Mr Barker's medical history."

"Maybe before, yeah, but I'm the one who dragged his arse here," Lucas said defiantly. "If I hadn't, those two pricks woulda left him passed out in the cemetery."

He had a point.

Henry sighed. "Can we speak of it over drinks? Please?"

Lucas's gaze flicked to the stairs. Was he thinking of the same thing Henry was in that moment? Reflecting on the last time they were together in the parlour? The memory of it stirred Henry's nerves uncomfortably, but Lucas relented. "Yeah, all right."

Henry escorted him to the parlour and left him there a moment while he went to Frederick's room. He felt badly for waking his butler in the dead of night, but Daniel's horse and wagon could not be left out in the alley unattended until morning.

When Henry returned, he poured Lucas a drink and refilled his own glass from earlier before having a seat. Lucas stared down at his gin, not making any attempt at eye contact. Henry had to admit, it was difficult to sit there across from him. Ruffled and tired, his hair mussed so that a few cinnamon-coloured strands swept across his forehead and into his eyes…

It made Henry wish that Lucas would kiss him again.

Henry, too, stared down at his drink, tracing his thumb along the rim of the glass. The silence in the room was tangible. After a spell, he took a deep breath. "I told you when I first met Daniel, he was ill."

Lucas paused, then nodded. "Same thing? Fits?"

"Seizures," Henry agreed. "I find *fits* to be such an unflattering term. He did quite a number on himself when it came on. Fell right into the middle of the street, broke his arm, suffered lacerations on his head."

"So…what, someone brought him to hospital?"

Henry shook his head. "We were both at the same public house that night. I found him as I was leaving. Everyone else likely just thought him drunk, but I knew better. As he came to, he begged me not to take him to hospital, so I brought him here instead."

The memory of that night still sat so vividly in Henry's mind. Now, it was difficult to picture Daniel frail, but at the time, even with his tall stature and fierce eyes, he'd seemed so vulnerable. He'd been alone in the world, despairing, and although it was the seizure that had him unconscious outside the tavern, he *had* been drunk too. Much of Daniel's life had come crashing down that evening. Henry had seen before him a man at the end of his rope, ready to hang.

Lucas worried at his bottom lip. "What is it, exactly? The fits—seizures. What causes them?"

"He began having epileptic episodes after an accident at a previous job, so my assumption would be it's a result of that head injury. We aren't certain if anything makes it worse, though extreme stress seems to bring it about more frequently."

And therein lay the biggest problem: work. Daniel *could* work. He was good at it, too. But no employer wanted someone around, operating heavy machinery, working aboard ships or in the mines, when that person could collapse at any given moment.

"Diggin' graves ain't exactly a stress-free profession," Lucas pointed out.

"No, it's not. But it permits him to work at his own pace and to have assistance, the opportunity for breaks when he needs them." Glass sighed, scratching a hand down his jaw. "When he began taking on more work, I cautioned him against that, but it's a difficult situation. He has medication that helps to some degree, but it comes with a rather hefty slew of side-effects and although it decreases the episodes, nothing rids him of them completely. He needs money to afford his medications and to live, but the more he works, the worse his condition appears to get."

Lucas slid a hand over his face. He sat in silence, nursing his drink and gazing into the fire. Henry granted him that quiet, allowing him to mentally unpack the undoubtedly stressful evening he'd been through. Henry would need to have a talk with Daniel about hiding such pertinent information from those he was working closely with; Lucas deserved to have avoided this fear. For that matter, Daniel was usually quite good at recognising the signs of when a seizure was coming upon him; it was rare for one to sneak up out of nowhere.

After emptying his glass, Lucas set it aside and moved himself to the edge of his seat. "I ought to be getting home. He's all right here for tonight?"

"Don't be ridiculous. It's the early hours of morning, no time to be traipsing across town. You're welcome to stay here."

"You got another spare room?" Lucas looked at him, and their eyes finally met, although only for a moment before Henry looked away again. Looking at Lucas in such a way made his resolve start to waver. It would have been so easy to give in, to simply open his own room for Lucas. Envisioning him there, sprawled out upon Henry's bed, sleeping soundly in his arms, was so tempting that it made his chest ache.

He swallowed hard. "No, I'm afraid not. But that bed is plenty big enough for the pair of you. Otherwise, you're welcome to the settee in here."

Lucas sighed, sounding almost...disappointed? Henry wasn't certain. "I'll stay with Barker, then. Thanks."

He rose to his feet, tugging his cap onto his head and moving for the door. Something about the sight of his retreating back made Henry's heart beat faster, a blind sort of panic bubbling inside him. He thought of Lucas leaving the other night. He thought of a day years ago when he'd watched a man he loved walk out of his life for the last time.

"Mr Walker? About that night..."

Lucas paused in the doorway. "It's fine. Whatever it was. Sorry for it and all that."

Henry stood, heart lodged in his throat. He took several long steps to cross the room, aching to turn Lucas around to him, to take his face in his hands. An ache he ignored, of course.

"You owe me no apology. In fact, I'm the one who ought to be apologising."

Lucas turned to him. "Sorry?"

Oh, where did he even begin? This wasn't a conversation he wanted to have, but the tension between them? He wanted that even less. "I have been alone for a very, very long time, in every sense of the word. So, please believe me when I say the blame for that night lies with me. I'm not good at maintaining friendships."

Lucas tipped his chin back, jaw set, eyes boring into Henry's in a way that made him want to flinch away. How did he explain to this man that they had too much going against them for anything like this to work? Henry was hardly worth the trouble. He never had been.

"Friendship, huh?" Lucas finally said, voice soft. "Not gonna pretend to know what goes through that head of yours. If you keep pushin' me away 'cause I'm no rich man or if it's just 'cause I'm a man at all. But you were at

The Duck that night. You've gone to pubs before, so some part of you is lonely and lookin' for something to fill that. When you're ready to actually accept what others are offering, maybe I'll still be around."

Henry opened his mouth, but the words wouldn't come out.

When he could only stare at Lucas, the younger man cut a thin, humourless smile, said, "G'night, Mr Glass," and stepped out of the room.

Was he right?

Henry had been struggling to maintain these boundaries between them, to not cross any lines, and he'd been failing miserably. He'd wanted to be a good friend to Lucas, someone he could turn to and rely on in the same way that Daniel did. If Henry couldn't have the love and relationship that he desired, having Lucas in his life in *some* form was better than nothing.

Henry wondered if he was only incapable of maintaining a friendship when his heart and body wanted more. Did romantic inclinations and attraction override his kindness, filtering it into something different, something painful?

He'd tried friendliness. He'd tried distance, too. He'd not permitted himself any time alone with Lucas after their kiss. That lack of contact had wounded Henry so deeply, far more than he'd ever have thought with someone he'd known only a few months.

If they could not find some sort of common ground to coexist with one another, Henry feared a repeat of fifteen years all over again. Back then, the idea of marrying, of watching the first man he loved marry, had seemed impossible, something that would have rendered his heart eternally broken. Having let Graham leave, however, now stood as the single biggest regret in Henry's life—and he would never lay eyes on the man again. That loss had left a hole in Henry's heart that he had been certain would never be filled, and only in retrospect had he realised that having Graham in his life, in any shape or form, would have been better than being ripped away entirely.

He wished he knew what the right path now was.

Henry listened to Lucas's footsteps carrying upstairs and into the spare room, the sound of the door opening and closing, the gentle creak of floorboards as he moved about and readied himself for bed. Henry returned to his chair and sat, poured himself another drink. Despite the late hour, he did not think he would be finding sleep anytime soon.

EIGHTEEN

Lucas woke to an empty bed, a clattering sound, and Barker swearing. When he opened his eyes and rolled over, he saw his roommate at the wash table, attempting to shave with shaky hands.

"Gonna slit your throat, mate," Lucas said around a yawn.

Barker peered at him in the mirror's reflection. "Maybe, but I'll be damned if I let someone else take a razor to my face."

With a roll of his eyes, Lucas slid out of bed and stretched. For the sake of Barker's pride, he didn't press the issue. "All right, then? Feeling better?"

Barker, having picked up the flat razor again, leaned to the mirror and seemed to struggle with keeping his hands steady as he dragged it across his jaw. He managed without cutting himself, at least. "Fine. Sorry about…about all that."

Bless him, he sounded so bloody awkward, and Lucas could only imagine the embarrassment he was harbouring. "No worries. Got your part of the payment, by the by. It's in your coat."

That made Barker stop. "How'd you manage that?"

"Told Fitch and Deacon I'd see to it they'd be up shit creek if they tried to stiff you on it, and for whatever reason, they believed me." He shrugged.

Barker turned to look at him, though his expression was unreadable. Lucas wasn't great at reading people to begin with, and Barker was a tightly shut book most of the time.

"What?" Lucas asked.

"Nothing. I just…" Barker took in a slow breath and turned away again. "Thank you, is all."

"You'd have done the same." He smiled to himself, knowing that without a doubt. Barker had a good heart. Lucas thought it was why Barker and Glass got on so well.

Lucas himself was still pretty sore at Glass, though he couldn't quite pin down why. Maybe because he knew damned well there was something holding up all those walls of his and Lucas couldn't figure out what. He'd stayed up late into the night thinking about it, dwelling on it. Clearly, the problem there wasn't disinterest on Henry Glass's part. So, then, what was it? Was it possible that although he fancied men, he'd never been with one? While peculiar to Lucas, who'd been with his share of men since he was fairly young, he'd encountered plenty of gents who never gave into their desires until well into their thirties and forties. Glass would not have been alone in that, if it were the case. Lucas almost wished that he'd asked.

Barker finished his shave, washed his face, and ran a brush through his curly hair. Even put-together, there was still something drawn about his face, something tired. He didn't look quite like himself. A residual effect of the seizure, Lucas wondered?

Lucas took a seat and hunched forward and watched the other man finish dressing, the slightly off manner of his movements. "So, them seizures…"

"Do we have to talk about it?" Barker straightened, turned to the mirror, and fussed with the buttons at the top of his shirt.

He frowned. "Yeah, actually, I'd like to. Some warnin' would've been nice. Also, how fuckin' daft was it for you to be going out on jobs with pricks like Fitch and Deacon? They'd have left you for dead in that cemetery, you know. Might've tossed you into that open grave and buried you."

"Likely would have," Barker solemnly agreed. "I told you, we were down a man. I always try to make sure someone I trust is around when I work, as much as I'm able. With Glass's group, it used to be Barnaby. With that group, a bloke named Richardson, but he recently moved his family out of London."

Lucas's eyes widened in realisation. "That was the reason you invited me, wasn't it?"

Barker's hands stilled for a moment, then resumed fumbling with the same button. "I trusted you not to leave me for the wolves if something happened."

Aside from Jasper, Lucas didn't have many friends. Oh, he had "friends," the sort he could have a laugh or a pint with, but honest-to-God *friends* whom he trusted? No, he'd always been in short supply of those. Until Barker said those words, Lucas wasn't sure he'd realised just how much that fact bothered him, because now his chest swelled with pride that this aloof, quiet man considered *him* trustworthy.

"Yeah, well, we're mates, ain't we?"

A twitch of a smile on Barker's mouth, there and gone as quickly as it appeared, told him he was right, although Barker insisted, "Don't get ahead of yourself."

Barker had just about finished readying himself for the day when a light knock at the door drew their attention and Glass stepped in. He brightened at the sight of Barker up and moving.

"Good morning, gentlemen. You look significantly more yourself, Daniel."

The other man frowned and scratched a hand back through his hair. "Sorry for the inconvenience."

Glass's gaze turned gentle. "I implore you to let me get some bromide from the hospital today. If money is that great of a concern—"

"It's not the money," Barker interrupted. He glanced at Lucas then and turned from them. "I've got my medicine. It's...more complicated than that."

"What more could there be?" Lucas asked.

Barker sighed, the sort of sigh that caught at the end, unsure if words would follow. But when Lucas and Glass only continued to stare at him, he relented. "The bromide… It slows the fits, sure. But it causes all sorts of new problems. It's fine for a few weeks, and then it's like my entire body starts to revolt. Shakes, headaches, I get confused. It's not that I can't afford it, or that I've stopped, just…" He shook his head. "Trying to find the right dosage for a good balance between it all, I guess."

Glass stepped forward and brought a hand to rest upon Barker's shoulder. "Side-effects are not uncommon with those medications. Worse for some people than others, of course, but any medicine in excess or for too long runs the risk of complications."

They fell into an uncomfortable silence, Barker clearly frustrated with his predicament, Lucas struggling to think of an answer. "There's really no other treatments?"

Glass scoffed. "Up until ten years ago or so, the only 'treatment' for epilepsy was to toss someone into the nearest asylum or get them an exorcism. Even now, many physicians are convinced it's a reflection of one's poor character. The deterioration of mankind is to blame, in their eyes."

Barker took a seat on the edge of the bed, elbows on his knees, pushing his hands through his hair. "It's fine. It's all fine. I'm used to it. It's the way of life for me, and I deal with it. I'm just sorry you two got caught up in it this time."

"Christ, shut it, will you?" Lucas, tone gentle despite the seemingly harsh words, sank down next to him. "We've got you. I'll go on whatever jobs you need me for, and I've got you. Right?"

When Barker lifted his head to look at him, it was not unlike looking into a mirror. Every offer of help Lucas had ever refused, every situation he'd made harder on himself because of his damned pride—it was all there in Daniel Barker's face. He realised then that Glass was a bit to Barker like Jasper was to Lucas: a friend desperate to help but not knowing how far to push.

But Lucas knew, because he and Barker were similar enough, so he added,

"It ain't up for debate, neither."

Barker's lashes lowered, resigned, but there was a twinge of quiet gratitude too. He patted Lucas's knee before standing. "I really ought to get home. You need a ride?"

"I can take him on my way into work," Glass interjected, and when Lucas cast him a puzzled look, he smiled sheepishly. "If Mr Walker has no objections."

"Suit yourself." Barker shrugged and swung on his jacket. To Lucas, he nodded, said they would talk soon regarding work, and then he slipped out through the door.

His absence felt like a tangible hole in the room, quickly filled with awkwardness at Lucas being alone with Henry Glass again. Lucas drew in a slow, calculated breath.

But Glass only gave him another of those quiet, bordering on shy smiles. "I need to finish getting ready. There is some leftover breakfast for you, if you'd like to grab something to eat."

He left without a further word, not giving Lucas a chance to ask him, *Why am I still here?*

Breakfast was indeed waiting for him when he went downstairs. Not only that, but Frederick also brought some of the leftovers bagged up to take home. "They'll go to waste here anyway," he said with a kind smile that Lucas returned.

During the carriage ride across town, Lucas devoured another scone, in part because it was delicious and in part to keep his mouth occupied so he had an excuse not to speak.

Glass didn't seem to get the hint about that latter bit, though, because he said, "I wonder if anyone has told you that you're a remarkable man, Mr Walker."

Ah. Unexpected conversation starter, that. Lucas swallowed the food in his mouth and kept his eyes down as he licked the crumbs from his fingertips.

"Not sure how you figure that."

"All things considered, you and Mr Barker don't know each other that well, yet you still went out on a limb for him." Glass tipped his head, studying Lucas with the utmost curiosity upon his face. "Not many would have done the same."

"He would've."

"Mr Barker is also quite remarkable in his own right, yes, but we're speaking about you."

"Why is that?" He crinkled closed the top of the paper sack and slouched into his seat. "For that matter, why are we here right now?"

"We're taking you home, and I'm going to work."

"I meant, why'd you offer to take me when I coulda gone along with Barker?"

Silence. One that dragged on long enough that Lucas looked over at Glass and found him studying his hands folded primly in his lap.

"What is it?" Lucas asked.

Glass closed his eyes. "I had hoped that I'd made it evident last night. I offered to drive you because I enjoy your company. I'm not certain I can give you a better answer than that."

It was a fair enough answer but frustrating, because what did it answer, really? *Why?* he wanted to ask. "*Why, because we're* 'friends'? *Why do you say things like that when all you're gonna do is shove me away after?*"

Then Glass jerked his head up and stared in surprise, and Lucas realised, horrified, that the question had actually left his lips. He'd opened his mouth and let the words fall out, to where they sat untouched on the seat between the two men, and Lucas would have gathered them up and swallowed them back down again if he were able.

The carriage rolled to a stop at an intersection. Lucas couldn't take it back, but he could run from it and from the rejection he knew was coming. He flung open the door, muttered a hasty thank-you and goodbye, and hopped outside, right into a damned puddle that soaked promptly through his trouser legs. He swore and skipped a few steps away.

Glass leaned out after him. "Lucas!"

He flinched at the sound of his given name on the other man's lips, at the way it tried to drag him back. He refused to let Glass keep doing this, tossing him out just to reel him back in again. It hurt too much. He yanked his cap further down onto his head and made a hasty retreat around the nearest corner.

The more distance, the better.

NINETEEN

"Sure you're feelin' all right?" Lucas pressed.

Barker didn't so much as look at him, instead surveying the unusually robust crowd at The Rusty Duck. "Stop it."

"Stop what?"

"Fretting. I'm fine."

Yes, he *seemed* fine, to Lucas. Back to his old self. But worrying was in Lucas's nature, and the idea that Barker could keel over again at any moment had him on edge.

They would need to find replacements for Deacon and Fitch, though. Not only did neither of them trust those idiots to have their back should such a thing happen again, but Lucas worried the pair might even turn on them. He could hold his own in a fight, and Barker looked like he could too, but Fitch and Deacon outweighed the both of them by a significant amount and Lucas wasn't up for nursing injuries if it could be avoided.

Work aside, getting an invitation for a bite to eat tonight, just some good company, was a pleasant surprise, and since he'd planned to come to The Duck that night anyway to see Jasper, it worked out well.

Speaking of…

He spotted the soft, dark tresses from across the tavern as Jasper wound his way through the throng of people towards them. Jasper had actually left his hair down, which was rare there at the pub. Too much unwanted attention, too many men who liked to touch it without asking, and, unless they were willing to pay, Jasper did not like strangers' hands on him.

He was all smiles as he approached, reaching out to tousle Lucas's hair fondly before falling gracefully into a chair at their table. "Look at you! You're dressed nicer every time I see you. Ah—Mr Barker, is it?"

Barker lifted his glass and gave a curt nod in greeting before returning his gaze elsewhere.

Lucas chuckled. "Pretty sure he's been eyein' that bloke over there. The one in the nice coat."

"Shut it."

Jasper leaned forward, following Barker's gaze. Which was, as it so happened, locked upon a rather handsome-looking red-haired gentleman engaged in conversation with a few others at the bar. Whatever they were talking about, the man clearly had his small group enrapt.

"Go talk to him?" Jasper suggested.

"I don't want to talk to him," Barker said, swivelling back around in his chair and finishing off his glass. "I want another drink."

Lucas gave his leg a nudge under the table and smiled when Barker glared at him. He wouldn't have anticipated that a person like Barker, who was so blunt and straightforward, would have reservations about approaching someone in a pub full of men just waiting to be approached.

Jasper was still studying Barker, though, with a certain sort of intensity that made Lucas a little nervous. Not interest, exactly. Whatever it was, he couldn't place it. At least until Jasper took a deep breath and asked, "You're the one Lucas has been working with, aren't you? Body-snatching?"

"Christ." Lucas immediately shot out a hand to clamp over Jasper's mouth. Never mind the words had already left it. "Don't talk about it here!"

Jasper peeled that hand away from his face. "No one heard me. I was only asking."

Barker watched him, likely debating just how much he cared to divulge to someone he'd met only once before. "That's right."

Jasper leaned forward, elbows on the table. "Is it safe?"

"Why, you want in on it?"

"Absolutely not. I just want to know that my friend is in good hands and not at risk of getting himself in trouble. He's had enough of that."

Barker cut a razor-thin smile. "Walker? In trouble? I can't imagine that."

"Fuck off, the both of you," Lucas muttered half-heartedly, not really minding. If his two mates got on with one another, all the better for him. Jasper and Barker could use more friends.

And their combined presence took some of the pressure off him to be sociable. As pleased as he was to spend time with them, he knew he had not been the best company over the last week since running out on Glass. For better or worse, he hadn't seen the man. Had even planned on turning down any jobs from him for the time being, one or two, just…for some distance.

Except Henry Glass hadn't called on them.

Lucas told himself it had nothing to do with their last conversation. A week was hardly unheard-of between jobs. It could be Glass had not finished with the previous body they'd delivered, or he'd become busy with work or the upcoming Christmas holiday, or any number of things. The world didn't revolve around Lucas, nor his relationship with Henry Glass.

Whatever sort of relationship that was, anyway. Every time he thought he'd figured it out, something happened to upend his expectations again.

Like Henry Glass just having walked into The Rusty Duck.

Lucas's spine stiffened, his shoulders pushed back. Barker took notice of the look on his face and followed his gaze. "Is that Glass?"

Lucas didn't respond. He pushed back his chair and sought to disappear into the crowd as swiftly as he could, with Jasper calling after him.

God, he was such a ridiculous coward. Glass could have been there for any number of reasons. Maybe he was looking for Barker. Maybe he just wanted a damned drink. Why did it matter if he saw Lucas there?

He wound through the other patrons, heading for the far back of the pub, towards the stairs leading up to the rented rooms. The only exit was the one Glass had come through, which meant leaving would require directly crossing into Glass's path. Lucas tucked himself around the corner near the stairwell, slumping against the wall and groaning. This was stupid. The Rusty Duck was *his* place, his stomping grounds. Why should he be cowering like this? Just because he was afraid of whatever confrontation might follow?

No, Glass wasn't really the confrontational sort. More like he'd pretend nothing was wrong, and somehow, the thought of that made Lucas's heart hurt even more.

Jasper popped his head around the corner after a moment, frowning when he spotted Lucas. "There you are! What was all that?"

Lucas thunked his head against the wall with a sigh. "Is he still out there?"

"Mr Barker went to speak with him. Why did you run?"

"I wasn't *runnin'*."

"Looked like it from where I was sitting."

He pulled a pout and crossed his arms. "Glass and I had an...awkward conversation last we saw each other, is all."

Jasper lifted his brows. "So, you had a bit of a row, and now you won't talk to him?"

"It wasn't a row, really."

"Then what was it?" When Lucas rolled his eyes and couldn't come up with a response, Jasper's lips parted in surprise. "Lucas Walker, you really do fancy him, don't you?"

Lucas's face jerked, levelling a dark look his way. Still, Lucas couldn't deny it. Not to Jasper. They could count on one hand the number of men Lucas had truly, honestly been attracted to beyond the occasional romp. This was different. Henry Glass was different. He was intelligent, kind, with a dry wit and sense of humour that Lucas adored...

And none of that mattered when Glass couldn't seem to make up his mind what the fuck he wanted—aside from, apparently, what he wanted not being Lucas.

Jasper seemed to take his silence as admittance. He brought a hand to rest upon Lucas's shoulder. "Oh, Lu. What haven't you been telling me?"

Lucas tipped his head back, studying the ceiling. The thought of opening his mouth and telling Jasper any of it seemed like too much. He didn't even know how to explain it. "It's stupid."

"It's not stupid, you—you stupid man." Jasper fumbled over his words and sighed, wrapping his fingers lightly about Lucas's wrist. "What's happened? If something's there, why won't you speak to him?"

"Because he's not interested, all right?" Lucas snapped. "We've been playing this game of back and forth for months now. He damned well knows. I've made it clear enough, and he's turned me away. What the fuck's a man like that going to want with someone like me, anyhow?"

Jasper's expression darkened then, his mouth downturned, and his hand shot up, grabbing hold of Lucas's chin. "Don't raise your bloody voice at me," he scolded sharply, and for a split second, the Welsh accent he tried so hard to smother when he spoke rang through brightly. "And don't you dare speak of yourself like that! Any man—rich or poor—would be lucky to have you. You're a good man with a good heart, Lucas Walker. If some foolish surgeon can't see that, then he isn't worth your time."

Lucas drew in a deep breath and swallowed back the lump forming in his throat. Jasper drew him forward then, into his arms, holding tight until Lucas gave in and returned the embrace. He wasn't certain what had sparked such a heated reaction from his friend, but he felt there was something more to it— as though Jasper was speaking those words to himself as much as to Lucas. That thought made him hug Jasper back even more tightly.

When the other man finally pulled away, he patted Lucas's cheek and smiled. "I've got a cull soon, so I need to be going. Will you be all right here with him?"

Yes. No. He wasn't sure. Casting aside that uncertainty, he offered a forced grin and the answer, "Go on."

Jasper took his leave. Lucas allowed the smile to fall from his face and closed his eyes, giving himself a few more moments before pushing away from the wall. If Barker had approached Glass, maybe the two of them would be busy conversing and Lucas could sneak past.

He steadied his nerves and peeked around the corner to scan the busy room. When his eyes finally landed on Glass, he was indeed in the company of Barker—except the two of them weren't alone. Another man that Lucas didn't recognise sat with them. Now and again, he could make out the profile of the stranger, the slope of his nose and the upturned corner of his mouth, smiling…right at Glass. A hand upon Glass's arm. Something he said made Glass laugh, and an ugly burst of jealousy flooded Lucas's veins.

Ridiculous. You've no right to be jealous.

Any thoughts he might've had about gathering his courage and approaching were tossed out with the bath water. Lucas skirted the edge of the room, making for the exit.

He didn't allow himself to look back.

TWENTY

The rain suited his mood, but certainly did not improve it. By the time Lucas reached his flat, his clothes were soaked through, and he had a case of the chills. As soon as the door shut behind him, he got a fire going in the stove and proceeded to pull off the wet garments. He put on a kettle for tea, fried up a couple of eggs, and ate a middle-of-the-night meal wearing only a pair of drawers while seated on his bed.

Moving around, doing things, meant his mind stayed off the topics he'd rather not think about. Such as how he'd overreacted at the pub. How he'd got ridiculously oversensitive seeing Glass so much as speak to another man—no matter how familiar the two had seemed, it wasn't Lucas's place. It wasn't his right.

But his insides were still in knots, and the eggs didn't sit well, and he lay in bed staring at the leaking roof, skirting around feelings of longing and trying to keep them at bay.

When someone knocked, he damned near leapt from bed, heart in his throat.

He threw open the door, still in nothing but his undergarments, and found himself staring at Barker, whose eyebrows immediately rose.

"Did I wake you?"

Why? Why in the hell had he thought for one bloody second that it would've been Henry Glass? Especially when Lucas would have about died if that man ever saw the sort of place he lived.

Crestfallen, Lucas took a step back to let Barker inside, out of the rain. "I was about to go to bed. What is it?"

Barker lifted a sizable parcel, wrapped in paper and tied with twine, and placed it upon the table. He'd managed to keep it dry, by the looks of it. "Since you decided to run off, Glass asked me if I'd deliver that to you."

Lucas studied the parcel, frowning. "What is it?"

"How would I know? None of my business." Still, he crossed his arms and watched, as though waiting for Lucas to open it so he could make it his business.

With a heavy sigh, Lucas stepped over to the table, pulling loose the twine and tearing through the parchment. Inside were several garments, crisp and new, folded with care, atop of which was a small card with the words *Mr Lucas Walker* and the emblem of a tailor shop stamped in the corner.

Barker leaned over. "What's all that?"

Lucas frowned. "That first job I went on with you? The next morning, Glass took me to get measured for some clothes. I'd forgotten all about them, honestly."

"That was a while ago. Why's he just now getting them to you?"

"Don't know." Lucas ran a hand over a blue silk waistcoat on the top of the pile, fingers grazing the buttons, the silver brocade... Surely the tailor shop hadn't taken this long to make these things, which meant Glass had been holding on to them for some reason or another. He lifted his head to look over at Barker. "This was it? He just asked you to deliver it?"

"Well, he's got a job for us on Saturday. But he and I were distracted with other conversation topics, so that was about it."

That earlier ugly feeling reared its head again. "Right. That bloke that was chatting him up, yeah?"

"What?" Barker paused. "Blackthorne, you mean?"

Lucas sniffed and began to look through the parcel's other contents. "Whatever his name is."

Barker's eyes remained locked on to him, and then he scoffed. "Are you fuckin' with me right now, Walker? Are you *sulking* because your lover was talking to someone else?"

"He is *not* my—"

"But you want him to be. Bloody hell, the two of you are infuriating." Barker shook his head and headed for the door.

Lucas squared his shoulders. "What's that supposed to mean?"

Barker opened the door and turned, spreading his arms wide. "It means that maybe you ought to *ask* him who that bloke was before making such an arse out of yourself."

He left without another word, and were Lucas not still in only his drawers, he might have followed the man for clarification.

He had overreacted. He'd known that from the moment it happened, yet it hadn't stopped the surge of insecurity and anger from coursing through him. Knowing his feelings were irrational and actually controlling them were two very different beasts. But if Barker was telling the truth, if there was a simple explanation for all of this… He was going to feel like even more of an arse. Though that was infinitely preferable to any alternative, as far as Lucas was concerned.

He looked back down at the stack of clothes and began to gather them so he could put them safely away. Glass's crew had an upcoming job, and now Lucas needed to think of a way to make up for his foolishness…and figure out how to properly say thank you.

TWENTY-ONE

Instead of going straight from home to meet up with Barker on Saturday night, Lucas caught dinner with Jasper at The Rusty Duck and proceeded to Glass's house afterwards. Frederick answered the door, seeming startled to see him there but inviting him in all the same. Rather than be ushered into the familiar dining room or parlour, Lucas was led through the kitchens and down into the cellar.

"Master Glass," the butler announced, "Mr Walker is here to see you."

As Frederick departed, Glass looked up from the autopsy table, empty save for papers and photographs, which he seemed to be in the process of organising. His jacket lay over the back of a nearby chair, and his sleeves were rolled to his elbows. Although his hair was done, he had a single stray curl that had defiantly worked itself free. All in all, it was quite a fetching look on him. Lucas wished he'd worn some of the nice things Glass had purchased for him, but he'd been unable to think of a reasonable excuse to do so that still would have enabled him to change into his normal work attire in a few hours.

"Mr Walker," Glass said with as much surprise as Frederick had evinced.

"Sorry to drop in unexpectedly," Lucas said, adjusting his cap. "I can come back, if you'd rather."

"No, no. Not at all." Glass set aside his pen and straightened his spine. "Is everything all right?"

"'Course it is. I just wanted to…"

And that was where Lucas floundered. Because he didn't know *why* he was there beyond wanting to thank Henry Glass again, to apologise for running out on him, or maybe just because— "I wanted to see you."

The words tumbled from his lips just as they had that day in the carriage, and if he'd been quick enough, witty enough, he could have made that comment sound casual and not laced with so much emotion that it clearly meant something much more. It wasn't *I wanted to see you so we could have a chat.* It was *I wanted to see you because I don't feel right when I'm not seeing you.*

Glass's expression softened. "And here I thought you were upset with me."

"I was. I am." Lucas rolled his shoulders back into a shrug, cramming his hands into his pockets.

"Then…?"

"Then—what? I owed you a thank-you for the clothes. And I thought we should—you and me. Maybe we ought to…talk." Lord, getting out the words was like shoving wet sand past his tongue.

Glass slowly circled the autopsy table at the end closest to Lucas, putting them much closer than Lucas had been prepared for. Lucas waited for the sort of evasiveness he'd come to expect from Glass, an excuse as to why they shouldn't be delving into this conversation. But Glass leaned onto the edge of the table, hands folded before himself, and said, "All right. Then let's talk."

"Fantastic." Lucas swallowed hard. He couldn't *not* look at Glass without making that obvious. Instead he found his gaze about level with the other man's chest, the small V-shaped area of flesh where his undone topmost shirt buttons lay him bare.

Lucas thought of all the things he'd played over in his head to say. *I have feelings for you. I want to be near you. I can't stand when you're so kind to me because that makes it harder when you don't want me here.*

I'm fairly certain I'm falling in love with you, and I don't know what to do.

"You ordered them clothes ages ago," he began.

Glass pursed his lips together. "I did."

"Why'd you wait so long to give 'em to me?"

"You seemed displeased after our trip to the tailor's, and then—" He faltered, clearing his throat. "And then that kiss happened, and things were a bit…strained between us. I thought such a gift would be unwelcome."

"Then why now?" Lucas pressed.

Glass took a slow, deep breath, chin dipping down towards his chest. Silence fell over the room and lingered so long Lucas thought he'd not get an answer at all, until, "I was in love with a man, once."

He looked as though he wanted to flee upstairs and never look back, Lucas thought. He'd never seen Henry look so anxious, so prepared to crawl out of his own skin over a conversation. Yet he was still here. Progress.

Lucas swallowed hard. "Yeah?"

"I was about your age, I suppose. Wide-eyed and hopeful, the world at my fingertips. Everything in my life was shaping up to be everything a man could have wanted." He smiled, fleeting and sad. "Then I met Graham."

Hearing him speak of another man like that, the look of longing and pain there in his face—Lucas waited for that earlier jealousy to rear its ugly head, but it remained dormant, instead replaced by a deep sense of regret and empathy for Henry. He did not dare interrupt.

"We met in a bookstore. I thought he was the most gorgeous creature I'd ever seen. We struck up a conversation, spent…oh, it must have been hours, poring over books and conversational topics. It was pouring outside, and we walked in the rain instead of catching a cab because we wanted that much longer in one another's company."

Lucas lowered his gaze. "So… Was he not—I mean…"

"He cared for me," Henry clarified. "My feelings were very much reciprocated. But the cost of being together was far too great. We both had such promising futures, and to sacrifice it all…"

Lucas could see where this was going. "He wasn't willing to risk that."

Henry's smile turned bitter, sad. "He was. I wasn't."

Lucas's eyes grew wide and snapped back to the other man's face.

"I might have been able to do it myself, but Graham... He'd worked so very hard for everything in his life. The idea that he might need to sacrifice anything to be with me—I did not see how it could be worth that for him. He left the city shortly after my engagement was announced, and I suspect he agreed to a match his own parents were pressing for him."

For some reason—pity, sadness, understanding—Lucas's eyes pricked with tears. He blinked them back. "Do you regret it now?"

"I've regretted it every day of my life, I suspect."

He ran a hand down his face. "What's that got to do with me and them clothes, then?"

Glass inclined his chin with a sigh. "It has to do with so much of my life and my choices being mired in guilt and regret. Giving you those clothes was rather a split decision on my part. I asked myself if I would regret it, never getting to see you wear the things I got for you, and the answer was yes."

A soft laugh fell from Lucas's throat. "Christ almighty. I had all these things memorised that I came here to say," he muttered and took a slow step closer, closing that already small gap between them. "Now you've gone and said all that, and I don't know where to start."

Glass straightened up the slightest bit but did not shy away from him. "Start with why you're displeased with me, perhaps."

His mind came up blank even for that. At least, until Glass's hand lifted to his face, cupped his cheek with the utmost delicacy that nearly drew a whimper from Lucas's lips. If he were a smarter man, he'd pull away until he fully understood what was happening.

If he were smarter.

" 'Cause every time I think I got you—us—figured out, you go and do something like that," Lucas managed, unable to help leaning into the touch, soaking it up for every second that he could. "I don't know what you want from me."

Glass's thumb slid across his cheekbone in a slow, affectionate swipe. "Oh, dear boy... I would never ask anything from you. Therein lies the problem, don't you see?"

Lucas opened his eyes and forced himself to look the other man in the face. "Because I'm younger?"

"In part," Glass admitted, lowering his lashes, eyeing Lucas's mouth when he spoke even as his tongue glanced across his own lower lip. "They're my own reservations, none of which have anything to do with you or—that is..."

"You're doing it again, is what's happening. You took that decision away from Graham, and you keep takin' it away from me." It made sense now that he thought about it. Every instance of Glass inching closer then running away. One step forward, two steps back.

Glass turned worried eyes to him, brows knitted together. "Yes. I suppose that's an accurate assessment."

Lucas shifted closer. "Then you really ought to stop it. I'm a grown man; my decisions are my own, and I think I've made it pretty damn clear that my decision is that I want you. So, what's your response to that gonna be?"

They stood so close that it would have been no effort at all for Lucas to kiss him. It took everything he had not to, to try to see if Glass could get the words out. When he didn't, when his gaze only continued to flick between Lucas's eyes and his lips, Lucas thought, *To hell with it*, and brought their mouths together.

Glass let out the most delightful, breathy groan into the kiss. The hand against Lucas's cheek slid up his jaw, around to cup the back of his neck and hold him right where he was. Something in the gesture, the applied pressure cradling the back of his skull, sent a pleasant jolt straight down into Lucas's groin. If he had only but a moment to enjoy this before Glass changed his mind again, then he'd take whatever he could get.

Lucas wound an arm around Glass's middle, inching forward, a shift of fabric against fabric as their bodies pressed flush together and, even through the material of their trousers, Lucas could feel him beginning to harden. His own cock twitched to attention, and he wondered how many levels of hell they'd be visiting if he yanked Glass's trousers down right then and there to suck him off in front of his autopsy table.

It was a glorious mental image behind his closed eyelids: the sounds of pleasure he could coax from the other man's lips, the taste of him spilling against the back of Lucas's tongue... He groaned outwardly at the thought, curling a hand against the small of Glass's back, and Glass canted his hips forward in response, making Lucas's mind go blissfully blank for a fraction of a second.

Somewhere in the house, a clock began to chime ten, and in unison something in the back of Lucas's head went off. He had somewhere to be, and he was running late now.

So, it was Lucas who pulled back this time, though not without a frustrated growl, even more so when he got a look at Glass's face, properly flushed and discombobulated, just the way Lucas wanted to see him.

"What's wrong?" Even Glass's voice came across delightfully rough and low, tinged with want.

Lucas managed a tight smile. "If you recall, you gave us a job to do. I've gotta meet up with Barker."

Glass blinked once, and then his eyes widened in realisation. "Oh. Oh— that's...yes. Probably for the best. Would you like Frederick to drive you? At least somewhere nearby?"

Lucas forced himself to back up a step. His prick strained against the confines of his trousers, protesting the sudden absence of friction and warmth. He idly wondered if he'd have time just to slip a hand into Glass's trousers and one into his own, to get them both off before he had to go, but like hell if he wanted that to be the memory of their first time.

"That would be helpful, actually." He licked his lips and adjusted his cap. "See you in a bit then, yeah?"

As he made to leave, Glass called out to him, almost tentatively. "Lucas?"

He turned.

Glass was a sight to behold, hands braced back against the table, aroused, cheeks pink even in the feeble lighting. And the way that he smiled, somewhere between uncertain but hopeful, made Lucas's heart skip a beat. "We'll continue this conversation later, I hope."

Lucas grinned. "That's a promise."

TWENTY-TWO

Frederick dropped him off a few blocks from the graveyard, leaving Lucas with enough time to meet Barker and Pendleton without being late. Barker took one look at him and cocked his head.

"You look chipper."

"Been a good night." Lucas hummed, taking up one of the shovels from Pendleton. "Let's get on with this, yeah?" The sooner they finished, the sooner he could get back to Glass and they could resume what they'd started.

The graveyard was shoddily fenced in, giving them multiple locations where they could have got in and out—a relief because it meant, if they needed to make a hasty retreat, they'd not have to worry about a single exit providing an escape.

Pendleton, Lucas noted, was abnormally quiet. Something in his entire demeanour was off, in fact, enough that Lucas asked, "You all right, mate?"

To which Pendleton only grunted a response and picked up his pace.

Odd, but they were hardly good enough acquaintances for Lucas to press the issue.

They located their appointed grave, and Barker took the first shift digging. Lucas crouched, rocking back on his haunches, and watched his friend for any sign of fatigue that suggested he might need a break or risk having another of his seizures. To his credit, Barker seemed to know just when to slow it down and pass the torch, which he did around the time Lucas insisted on taking over. They swapped places, and Lucas dug in. Literally.

Barker sat down in the slushy grass, hands braced behind him, and head tipped back as he caught his breath. Lucas was so focused on the task at hand that he didn't notice they were short a person until he turned to pass the shovel off.

"Hey—where's Pendleton?"

Barker lifted his head and blinked tiredly. They looked around, finding no sign of their third member. The sack and one of their lanterns were gone. Lucas hauled himself out of the grave, a sense of unease crawling beneath his skin, pumped through his veins quickly by his racing heart.

"I think we should go," Barker said quietly.

Lucas wet his lips and nodded in agreement.

No sooner had Barker snatched up the remaining lamp from the ground than a constable stepped out from the trees nearby and grabbed him. He shouted, panicked, and promptly began to struggle. Lucas abandoned the shovel and dove for him but found himself snagged by another two uniformed men, who shoved him to the ground, granting him a face full of dirty, half-melted snow.

"The pair of you are under arrest," one of the constables sneered, pressing a knee into Lucas's spine while another twisted his arms behind him.

His mind spun. This wasn't right. These men hadn't been patrolling; they'd been hiding. They'd been *waiting.*

He swore under his breath, twisting his head to try to get a look at Barker, who was still straining against the man attempting to get him to the ground. He was a wiry thing, and the constable couldn't seem to get a good enough grip on him to shackle him—which was precisely what the other two were presently doing to Lucas's wrists.

Then Barker stilled. Just like that, he went limp in the constable's arms, sagging to the ground so swiftly that he damned near dropped him.

Lucas's stomach sank.

No, no, no...

"What's going on?" the constable yelped, staring down at Barker's now prone body like he wasn't certain whether he ought to take the opportunity to restrain him or if something had gone horribly wrong. When Barker began to seize, the constable abruptly scrambled back, hands up, eyes wide. A sandy-haired bloke grabbed Lucas's chin and jerked it towards Barker, as though he wasn't already watching in abject horror.

"What's wrong with him?!" the man demanded.

"What's it look like? He's havin' a bloody fit!" Lucas snarled back. "Let me up! Give him space!"

They did give him space, but no one moved to let Lucas go to him. He bucked against their hands with a swear, only to have them haul him to his feet and turn him around.

"Get this one to the wagon," the sandy-haired officer instructed the other two, who began to shove him away from the grave. Lucas tried to twist in their grasp.

"You don't understand; you gotta put him on his side, don't just—"

One of the men cuffed him across the back of the head, not hard enough to render him unconscious but hard enough to make him stumble, to see stars and damn near bite off the tip of his own tongue. The taste of blood swam into his mouth, and he coughed on it.

It wasn't until they were nearly out of the cemetery that Lucas's head began to clear, but there was little he could do about his predicament. The constables shoved him into the back of their patrol wagon, securing the doors behind him and leaving him shrouded in darkness. Only a small, barred window gave him access to the outside, but its allotment of light was pitiful. Nevertheless, Lucas pressed his face to it, desperate to get a look back the way they'd come, to see Barker.

No such luck. Before the other two constables could even go back to their partner, he came stumbling towards them, a string of curses in his wake.

"Fucker got away!"

"What d'ye mean he got away? Wasn't he havin' a fit?"

"Well, recovered right quick, obviously! Or else he was fakin' it."

Lucas slumped against the wall, heaving a sigh of relief. Barker was all right. He'd got away safe. Good.

The officers groused amongst themselves a few moments longer before they loaded onto the carriage and it began to move. It finally occurred to Lucas he ought to be concerned for his own well-being. He was getting arrested—though what the charges were exactly, they'd yet to tell him.

There was nothing doing now, though, except to close his eyes and wait out the ride. It was going to be all right. They'd give him a slap on the wrist, maybe throw him in a cell overnight, and he'd be let out come morning.

He lost track of time. It could have been ten minutes or an hour before they came to a halt and unlocked the doors to yank Lucas out, not bothering to be gentle as they manhandled him into the police station. He winced at the wrenching of his shoulders, the sharp jab of a palm between his scapula, and the knot forming on the back of his skull where he'd been clubbed earlier.

They sat him on a bench, and a sergeant circled a desk to approach, arms folded and bushy eyebrows raised. "Well, this is him, is it? Where's the other? I thought he said there'd be two."

He said? Lucas narrowed his eyes.

"The other one, er, got away," the sandy-haired constable admitted.

The sergeant groaned. "Can't have you do anything right, can I, Harris? Go make yourself useful and get a report written up."

Constable Harris's cheeks went cherry red, and he shuffled off.

The sergeant looked back down at Lucas. "Which one are you, then, lad? Mr Barker or Mr Walker?"

Pendleton. Pendleton sold us out, Lucas sneered to himself. He was going to break that man's fucking jaw when next they saw each other. "What's my crime, exactly, sir?"

"Your crime," the sergeant said patiently, "is theft."

"Funny, 'cause I ain't stolen a thing."

The sergeant smirked. "No? Then what's this?" He lifted a hand, a silver pocket watch dangling from his fingers. Lucas frowned.

"What is that?"

"This was buried with the man you just dug up."

"That's not possible—we didn't even get his coffin open!"

The sergeant looked to the other two constables, one of whom shrugged. "Looked open to us, sir."

All the colour drained from Lucas's face. As he'd feared months ago, the police didn't need to have a real reason to prosecute. They could make one up. Who was a magistrate going to believe, seasoned officers of the law or some rabble-rouser from the slums?

"This ain't right. I never stole nothin' from no one, I swear!"

"Lock him up," the sergeant said, cheerful, with a dismissive wave. "And make sure our informant gets his money."

TWENTY-THREE

Henry's mind had not stopped reeling since Lucas left. He teetered between joy and panic, happiness at having got a taste of something he so desperately wanted, and fear that, somehow, his actions were going to be cause for regret later. But Lucas had been correct: fifteen years ago, he had denied the man he loved the ability to make his own choice and had regretted it every day since. It was time for Henry to loosen his hold on the reins; he could not control everything—particularly the decisions of others.

He was left to mull over those thoughts in the silence of his home. The people in his employ had long since left for the day, except Frederick, the only one who lived on-site, who had retired to his bedchambers off the kitchen. Henry himself would have ordinarily caught a few hours of sleep while awaiting the return of Barker's group, but he found himself pacing the length of his own room in his nightclothes and dressing gown, his mind running far too fast for sleep ever to hope to catch up with it. Now and again, Hilda lifted her head and whined at his restlessness from where she slept at the foot of his bed.

He thought of all the things he planned to say to Lucas upon his return. An apology, first and foremost, he thought. And then he wanted to take Lucas's face in his hands and kiss the man quite senseless, to tell him that he'd never need to want for anything again and that Henry's home was Lucas's home—if it would please him.

The technical details could be worked out. He would tell people he'd hired Lucas on for work around the house. Beyond that, it was hardly anyone's business. Perhaps it would be difficult; perhaps it would raise questions, perhaps, perhaps...

Henry was bound and determined not to let every *what-if* and *perhaps* frighten him into a corner again.

When it became too apparent that he'd not be getting any sleep, Henry retreated to the parlour downstairs with a book, Hilda, and a glass of wine by the fire. Best to settle his nerves before the others returned.

He'd become quite engrossed in his reading when a sudden pounding below tore him away from the words on the page and back to the world around him. A look at the grandfather clock told him that it was too soon for them to be back, and the last time someone had arrived at the cellar door with such urgency, it had been Lucas with a barely conscious Daniel.

With equal urgency, Henry abandoned his tome, shooed the dog from his lap, and hurried to throw open the cellar door. The first thing that crossed his mind upon seeing Daniel's face was relief that he was all right, and the second thing was that Daniel looked as though he'd seen a ghost.

"Daniel! What's happened? Are you all right?"

Daniel pushed past him to get out of the drizzling rain. The man was short of breath, as though he'd run the entire way here, except Henry could see the horse and wagon outside.

"We got caught," Daniel said. "They've got Walker."

Henry's heart about stopped in his chest. He shut the door, keeping a hand braced against it to steady himself as the world momentarily spun around him. Surely, he'd misheard—except, when he dropped his gaze, he saw Lucas's all too familiar cap, unfamiliarly gripped in Daniel's tight fist. "What?"

Dragging in a breath, Daniel pushed a hand through his hair. He was a calm man. A logical one. The sort who kept his wits about him through all manner of stressful situations. Never before had Henry seen him look so frazzled. Despite his even-keeled tone, he couldn't seem to stand still.

"I don't know. It was Pendleton, I think. We were digging, then he was gone, and the next thing we knew, a couple of bobbies were on us."

Henry stepped over to him, catching Daniel's face in his palms, studying him in concern. Daniel went still and stared down at him. His eyes were clear, steady, no sign of unwellness. Thank the Lord.

"How did you escape capture?" Henry asked.

"I feigned a fit," he admitted without the slightest bit of shame. "I made a run for it when their guard was down. I'm so sorry, Henry; there was no way for me to get us both out."

A brilliant method of escape, truth be told. "Everything will be fine. Come, let's get you upstairs and dried off and a drink to soothe your nerves."

Daniel's shoulders slumped. He excused himself to slip back into the rain long enough to relocate the horse and cart in the nearby stables utilised by the houses on the row. The pair then retreated upstairs so Daniel could fill him in on the details of what had transpired.

Of course Henry was worried sick; it felt like something had physically lodged itself in his throat. But part of who he was as a person—as a surgeon— knew how to remain calm under pressure and think things through rationally.

Logic told him that if Lucas had managed to escape on his own, then he'd show up at Henry's doorstep soon enough. If he'd been arrested…it was possible he'd simply spend the night in a holding cell and be released in the morning, if the police were feeling kind.

If they weren't? Well, then it would be time to really worry.

TWENTY-FOUR

Lucas hadn't eaten in three days. The first meal they served him tasted foul, and the bread was damned near stale enough to beat a man bloody with. When an officer returned and saw the bowl of gruel still full, he'd said, "Fine, if it ain't good enough for *his majesty*, I'll see you aren't offended by it again." And that was the last Lucas saw of food.

His stomach roiled furiously, and his throat was cracked and dry, desperate for water. He'd managed to get a few measly drops from a leak in the corner of the cell. It'd tasted of dirt and rust, but it'd been better than nothing.

How long were they planning on keeping him there? Had they gone back and hunted down Barker? They obviously had his name; even if he'd escaped the cemetery, they could have simply gone to his home and arrested him there. For that matter, what had Glass done when he'd learned of what had happened? *If* he'd learned at all? What about Jasper? He was going to be worried sick—and so cross with him. Lucas almost laughed at the *I told you so!* he could hear vividly in his head.

But worse than how his companions would react was the looming unknown. If convicted, there was no telling what punishment he'd receive. He'd seen men given six months of hard labour just for swiping a loaf of bread and another bloke given five years of penal servitude for receiving a couple of stolen pigeons. All Lucas knew was that he'd be viewed as a man committing a horrendous sin by desecrating a grave, and the magistrates would keep that in mind when deciding his punishment for allegedly stealing a watch he'd never seen in his life.

On the third day, Sergeant Kahn—Lucas had learned the name at some point during his stay—sent for him. But rather than being transported to have a chat with a magistrate about whether there was sufficient evidence for a trial, Lucas found himself being shoved back into another wagon while Kahn called to the driver, "Straight to the gaols."

What?

Lucas threw himself against the doors, cheek pressed to the bars while shouting out to Kahn. "Oi! What're you talkin' about? I'm supposed to go see the magistrate!"

Kahn turned and sneered at him, leaning in close. "Magistrate's busy. Figured a sodomite like you would enjoy some time in the gaols before havin' his case heard."

The wagon began to roll away from the curb, and Lucas's insides twisted, dread dropping like a stone into his belly. He had spent the last few days wondering what the hell had these officers so determined to prosecute him for something so minor, and he supposed this answered it.

Pendleton hadn't only sold him and Barker out for grave robbing but as sodomites, too. *That* wasn't a crime the sergeant had proof of, however, so he'd throw his full weight behind this measly larceny charge and hope it stuck. The problem was that it very well *could.*

And there wasn't a damned thing Lucas could do about it.

TWENTY-FIVE

They heard not a word from or about Lucas for days.

Henry himself could not go to the police station to inquire. They would have put two and two together, realised that Lucas had been grave robbing on his behalf, and that would have brought about even more trouble. And because Daniel was currently a wanted man, he was not a viable candidate to go either.

The task fell upon the young man Lucas had told him about some time ago, Jasper Rees. Although Henry had not met him, Daniel had, and he assured Henry that the lad was worried sick about his friend and would be as determined as they were to see him released.

Except when Mr Rees arrived at the police station and proceeded to question the constables there about Lucas, they practically laughed him out of the building. He returned to Daniel, near tears in his frustration. Daniel came by the hospital to relay this information to Henry. By then, Lucas had been gone for nearly a week, and Henry's ability to remain calm had severely worn thin.

If the law intended on playing difficult, Henry decided, so could he.

He sat down at the table in the back room of the hospital, the same where he'd sat across from Lucas all those months ago and asked him to dinner, and now wrote a swift note on a piece of paper. He folded and addressed it, then slipped it across the table to Daniel, who frowned.

"What's this?"

"A letter." He folded his hands together. "If you'd be so kind as to deliver that to Mr Blackthorne's office. The address is on the top there; it's only a few blocks away."

Daniel tucked the note into his pocket, a frown working across his face. "Mr Blackthorne? From The Rusty Duck?"

"We'll not get far in this endeavour without the help of a professional, I think," Henry said, and Daniel didn't argue with him on it.

By the end of the following day, he received word back from Theseus Blackthorne, agreeing to come meet the next evening. In turn, Henry sent word to Daniel. It seemed important that Blackthorne hear the story directly… if he was even willing to help.

Henry had operated on and saved the life of Blackthorne's elder brother some time ago, and in his gratitude, Blackthorne had assured Henry that if ever the need arose for a well-known lawyer, he would gladly assist. Henry had only been performing his job, however, with hospital compensation, and to call upon an advocate as though there were still some debt to be repaid? This plan could crumble to dust in his hands as swiftly as he'd formulated it.

Blackthorne arrived precisely on time the next night. Frederick showed him into the sitting room where Henry awaited. He stood with a smile that felt forced—all of his smiles this last week had—and extended a hand.

"Mr Blackthorne, I can't thank you enough for coming on such short notice."

Blackthorne was, as always, immaculately dressed. The emerald of his waistcoat set off the green of his eyes, accented the endless freckles across his face and the red of his neatly styled hair. Theseus Blackthorne hardly looked like the sort of man who had any interest in the law; he came from an exceptionally wealthy family, and his law practice was something he did out of boredom rather than necessity. But he was *very* good at what he did. Henry was hedging his bets on that.

"My apologies that I couldn't come last night," Blackthorne said, gripping Henry's hand and giving it a firm shake. "I had business I couldn't get away from."

Henry inclined his head, gesturing for the redhead to make himself comfortable. "I appreciate you coming at all. I know you're a busy man. Would you like a drink?"

"Please. Your letter sounded quite urgent." Blackthorne sank down into one of the upholstered chairs near the fire, lounging back, crossing his long legs elegantly.

"It is. I'm afraid a situation has arisen regarding one of my employees." Henry stepped to the bar cart, selecting one of his finer wines. For as well-off as he was in his profession, anything he had likely could not hold a candle to what someone from the Blackthorne family was used to.

"I don't suppose you're referring to your house staff?"

"No." He turned, offered the glass out, and sat with his own. "One of the men who has been procuring specimens for my research."

Henry clearly didn't even need to explain what he meant by that statement. There was a pause from Blackthorne, a raised eyebrow, as he took a drink. "I see. He was caught?"

"Yes."

"And you need the charges dropped."

"Yes. He was taken nearly a week ago, and we've not heard any word regarding him. The police refuse to answer any of our questions."

Blackthorne lowered his glass, tapping a finger against the rim of it. "I believe I told you, when you were successful with my brother's surgery, that I considered it a debt I would repay."

Henry swallowed hard, hopeful. "I remember."

"I'm one of the best lawyers this city has." There was no arrogance in his voice, only simple fact. Yet his gaze was so intense, focused on Henry, as though he could come to some interior conclusion just by the look upon the other man's face. "I'm also very busy and not prone to offering favours."

Henry did his best not to flinch inwardly. "I'm aware."

"And you wish to call in this favour for—what? How long have you known this lad, Mr Glass? What could an employee mean to you in a position that no doubt sees much turnover?"

"I'm not certain why that matters."

Blackthorne sighed, took another drink, and placed his glass aside. "I'm not a man who takes cases because someone needs me. I want to know why this is important to you before I decide whether or not it's worth my time and effort when I could be working for a paying client."

A frown tugged at Henry's face. "If payment is the issue, I can pay you."

Theseus chuckled. "You couldn't afford me."

Heat flushed Henry's face. It was a true enough statement, though he also knew for a fact that Blackthorne frequently did cases for little to nothing in return. This was a matter of appealing to his interests, not his bank accounts. "I'm a private man, Mr Blackthorne."

Certainly, the two of them were not *friends*, exactly, but good enough acquaintances with a common thread between them in their preferences. Blackthorne spread his hands wide.

"Please don't take any of this as an insult. I'm not trying to be difficult. This is merely my process for any client."

Henry sighed, shoulders slumping as he willed himself to relax. "I apologise. I've been rather on edge."

"It's understandable. And I do wish to assure you that, even if I would technically be representing your employee, *you* would be my client. Anything you say to me will be held in the strictest of confidences."

He felt he needed several more drinks in him for this conversation. Henry dipped his chin towards his chest, letting his gaze focus on the intricate patterns woven into the rug between their chairs. "Mr Walker is…someone I care about. Far more than I should."

Was that enough? Did he need to spell it out in any simpler terms?

Blackthorne was quiet for a moment, likely considering his response. "It will not be an easy matter. Particularly since the Yard seems to have it out for your companion, for whatever reason."

Henry lifted his gaze, hopeful. "But you think it can be handled?"

The other man scoffed. "Is that doubt I hear?"

A smile tugged at Henry's mouth. "I have no doubt that you are Lucas's best chance for a hasty release. Does this mean you'll take the case?"

Blackthorne's grin was slow and sweet, almost calculating. "I told you that I owed you a debt of gratitude, didn't I? I always pay my debts."

It dawned on Henry that Blackthorne had already made his decision prior to even stepping through the front door.

Speaking of the front door—the sound of a knock reached Henry's ears. Mr Blackthorne looked to him curiously, and Henry rose from his seat to pour a third glass. "That would be Mr Barker. I've asked him to come by to give you his account of what happened."

"Mr Barker?" Blackthorne repeated. Henry noted that he sat up straighter, lifting a hand as if to assure that his hair had not become unkempt. Interesting.

Frederick showed Daniel in not a moment later, and with equal interest, Henry also noted that Daniel had dressed himself quite finely indeed and that he'd made a valiant effort at taming those wild curls of his. He stepped into the room, and there was a moment when Daniel's eyes met Blackthorne's and Henry almost felt as though he didn't exist to either of them.

He raised his eyebrows. "Mr Barker, I'm glad you could make it."

Daniel started, clearing his throat. "Yeah, of course. Sorry I'm late; I walked."

Henry offered him a glass as he took a seat in the chair beside Blackthorne, who twisted slightly, leaning on his elbow towards Daniel. The shift in Blackthorne's body language was subtle, but Henry took notice.

"Mr Glass tells me you have information pertaining to the case. I presume you were with Mr Walker when he was taken?"

"I was," Daniel agreed.

He proceeded to recount the evening, with Blackthorne interjecting now and again to ask clarifying questions. The story unfolded in far greater detail than Henry had previously been given, enough that when he closed his eyes, he could almost picture the events playing behind his eyelids.

When Daniel finished, Blackthorne asked, "Since then, you've been unable to learn more from the Yard about his case?"

"Correct," Henry said. "We have an acquaintance—a friend of Lucas's—who has been attempting to get information, but the Yard has been less than cooperative. What I don't understand is *why*. Surely, they have much worse offenders than a couple of grave robbers."

Daniel sighed. "I can shed some light on that, I think."

Henry and Blackthorne looked at him curiously.

He started to run a hand through his hair, stopped, seemed to recall he'd styled it to lie as flat and tame as he could, and dropped that hand back to the arm of the chair. "I've been staying at The Rusty Duck to avoid the authorities, and I ran into Pendleton there the other night. We…had a few words."

"How many words before you beat him bloody?" Henry asked dryly. He knew Daniel. And no matter how even-keeled the other man was, he had no patience for men who wronged him—or wronged those he cared for.

Daniel gave a bit of a grunt and diverted his gaze to the fire, not seeing the curious look Blackthorne cast his way.

His face was drawn and tired, Henry thought, uncertain how to inquire after his friend's health with someone else present.

"He confirmed what we already knew," Daniel said, "that he'd been acting as an informant for the bobbies. They've been paying him for some time to turn over the names of the resurrectionists in the city, dismantling some of the larger groups."

Henry frowned. "Which leads back to my earlier question: why obsess over two solitary men when they have entire organisations to concern themselves with?"

"I suspect because, after doing this a while, he's run low on people to turn over. He made things up, no doubt saying we have connections that we don't have. And"—Daniel lifted the glass to his lips, draining it in one impressive fell swoop—"he told them about Walker and me. That we're *sodomites*. Naturally, that piqued their interest."

Silence befell the room for a spell, Henry taking that information in. It felt like a personal attack. He and Daniel had trusted Allan Pendleton, had thought that because he was *like them*, they had...what, some sort of understanding? A bond? How foolish. Now it had come back to bite them.

"Fantastic," Blackthorne finally muttered. "Well, grant me a few days, if you would. I will see what I can find out about Mr Walker's whereabouts, and we'll devise a strategy from there."

He stood, dipping his head, then turned to Daniel with a saccharine smile. "Mr Barker, could I interest you in a ride home?"

Daniel looked up at him, expression unreadable. "If it wouldn't be too much trouble. I don't fancy a walk home in the rain at this hour."

Henry rose, seeing his two guests to the front door to fetch their coats and Blackthorne's hat. He was loath for them to go; as difficult as it was to maintain decorum and be sociable, feeling productive—no matter how little—was preferable to sitting around alone and dwelling.

Daniel descended the steps towards the street, but Blackthorne stopped and turned to look at Henry. Perhaps it was the expression on his face, not hidden as well as Henry meant for it to be, because the redhead gave him something close to a sympathetic look and touched a hand to his shoulder.

"Please don't lose heart, my friend. This will be an uphill battle to fight, but it will most definitely be a battle we'll be prepared for."

TWENTY-SIX

The last time he'd been imprisoned, Lucas had spent a few days in a cell—but not like this. Not in an actual prison. He knew plenty of men who had, however, and none of them had had the most glorious of things to say about their time behind those stone walls.

After arriving at the gaols, it was quickly clear why.

Meals consisted of a few ounces of meat and potatoes, some gruel for breakfast, maybe a bit of cocoa if he was lucky. Everything he did, from the time they woke him at six o'clock in the morning until the time they made him go to bed at nine in the evening, operated on a strict schedule. Half an hour for meals, amidst work, chapel, exercise, work, more work...

The only reprieve came in the form of an hour just before bed. A single hour wherein he was permitted to write or read. More than once, he sat down to pen letters to Jasper, Barker, or Glass, but he feared his captors reading those, his friends suffering because of their association with him. Still, every day he listened to the guards call out names for mail, reminding himself that he did not want his friends to put themselves at risk, either.

What should have been no more than a few days' stay rolled into a week, and then two. It wasn't until week three that anything arrived in the post for him, and it was penned in unfamiliar writing with an equally unfamiliar name.

To Mr Lucas Walker,

I have been appointed your advocate for this case and will be at your side to represent you in the upcoming petty sessions, where we shall plead your defence to the magistrates.

Please do not lose hope. All will be well.

Sincerely,

Theseus Blackthorne

He read the letter again and again. An advocate? He certainly couldn't have afforded one. He'd fully planned on having to plead his own case—if they ever allowed him out of here to do so. But if someone had sought out a lawyer for him, only one person in his life could have done it.

Bless you, Henry Glass, he thought. And then he curled up on his side on the uncomfortable platform that served as his bed and slept better than he had in weeks.

TWENTY-SEVEN

"You look nervous."

Henry glanced across the carriage to Blackthorne. Henry realized he'd been gripping the head of his cane so tightly that his knuckles ached, and he had to force them to uncurl, to stretch the stiffness out of them. "Do I?"

"Quite."

He let out a breath and returned his attention to the scenery passing outside the window. In his pocket, he carried with him notes he'd compiled over the last few weeks as a result of his meetings with Mr Blackthorne, Daniel, and Mr Rees. Their story, their plans, laid out in careful detail. His own role was small, and the notes were not necessary, but having them there felt reassuring somehow. "I think nervousness would be natural in this situation."

Blackthorne agreed. "It is. Useless, though."

"Have you ever lost a case, Mr Blackthorne?"

To his surprise, the other man didn't hesitate to say, "I have. Many, actually. Is that surprising? Plenty of wealthy clients willing to dispense money for unwinnable cases."

"You simply seem so confident, as though nothing could go wrong."

"Something could always go wrong, my friend. But I don't think it will."

Henry wished he could share that assuredness, to take comfort in it. He'd no doubt have slept better in the nights leading up to this moment. "Your case is built on several people distorting the truth, you realise."

Blackthorne smiled. "Lying, you mean. Let's call it what it is."

"Lying, then. Several people who must lie, keep their stories straight under questioning."

"Yes."

"That doesn't concern you?"

"Not in the slightest."

Henry bit back a sigh.

"Mr Glass, please." Blackthorne leaned forward, pinning him with that intense look again, the one that commanded full attention and left Henry feeling as though Blackthorne could dig every last secret out of him. "I know the stress you're under, but have faith in me. I know what I'm doing. The constables may have a grudge against Mr Walker, but the magistrates overseeing these petty sessions are not going to be swayed by hearsay. The Yard may try to produce evidence of the grave robbing and theft, but, should the prosecution attempt to throw the accusation of buggery into the mix, our story will counteract it swiftly."

Holding his gaze, Henry struggled to rein in his worry.

The past several weeks had been miserable, full of never-ending apprehension and dread, all compounded by the fact that he hadn't a clue if Lucas was well or what must have been going through his mind, locked away in the gaols. Were his captors being rough with him? Did Lucas blame Henry for his plight? Henry had been so desperate to go see him, to try to get a letter through to him, but of course Blackthorne had advised strongly against it.

Henry asked, "Do you do this often? Lie in court?"

Blackthorne's features scrunched up briefly. "Not unless I must."

"How do you decide what constitutes a *must*?"

"When I think the law is wrong," he replied easily.

Henry's eyebrows lifted. "And are you a judge of such things, then?"

"I believe we all should be, to some degree."

"What degree is that, Mr Blackthorne?"

"You're full of questions today," Blackthorne responded with a laugh. "But no matter, if it takes your mind off other worries. When the law is used to punish someone good, someone who means no harm, *that* is when I'm willing to lie."

Henry was a little surprised; it went against what most attorneys would have said, which was to uphold the truth at any cost. "You do not consider body-snatching to be harmful?"

That earned him a scoff. "Why would I?"

"There are those who say that the desecration of the grave is an unforgivable sin, that the disruption of a body laid to rest will prevent that person's soul from moving on."

Blackthorne looked as though he was barely refraining from rolling his eyes. "If there is a God and he deems those people unworthy of his grace because their empty shells were used to better medicine and save others, then perhaps we're all better off having our graves desecrated."

Henry surprised Blackthorne and himself by laughing. "I see why Mr Barker has become so taken with you. That sounds very much like something he would say." Like something Daniel had, in fact, told him before. The man might have been brought up in a religious home, but he'd never had much in the way of faith himself, from what Henry could gather.

Blackthorne's smile was slow, pleased. "I suppose there are many reasons Mr Barker is so taken with me, my logic among them."

Henry would be a liar if he said he wasn't quite curious, wanting to pin down and put a label upon whatever had been going on between Daniel and Blackthorne. It would not have been entirely out of line; they were both his friends, both of value to him.

He refrained, however. At the end of the day, it was not any of his business, and he'd not be willing to divulge personal details of his own in exchange—particularly involving Lucas. "I'm infinitely grateful for both of you. Your assistance is invaluable."

The carriage slowed to a stop, and the footman dismounted to open the door for them. Blackthorne gave his knee a pat. "Come along, Mr Glass. Let's meet up with our companions. We have a case to win."

TWENTY-EIGHT

After the letter arrived from his advocate, only two more days passed before Lucas finally found himself loaded into another wagon and transported to the courthouse, shuffled inside—with his hands shackled in front of him this time, which allowed for much easier movement—and stood before two magistrates.

The room smelled of piss and sewage, air pumped from outside in a feeble attempt to better ventilate the otherwise stuffy space. It was crowded with onlookers present to witness the proceedings of a loved one. Also in attendance were Sergeant Kahn and one of the constables from that night, as well as a man Lucas suspected was the prosecutor.

The last time he'd been in this position, Lucas had narrowly escaped with his freedom. He wasn't certain he'd be so lucky this time, even if Glass's advocate showed. Lucas's hands quaked. All he had was his word he'd not been involved in thievery—and he had to hope these two men would believe him. The fact that he *was* guilty of desecrating a grave was not likely to win their favour. As it was, the magistrates peered at him, already with calculating stares, making up their minds about him without a word ever being spoken.

One of the justices squinted at Lucas. "Mr Lucas Walker, is it?"

Lucas swallowed hard past a dry throat. "Yes, sir."

"Have you an advocate present?"

"I… Um." He cast a look about the room, helpless. What did this Mr Blackthorne even look like? Would he really be there?

"Present, sir," came an unfamiliar voice from the back of the bustling room.

Lucas twisted around and saw a freckled-faced man with red hair and a sharp suit strolling down the centre aisle through the crowd.

"Mr Blackthorne," the same magistrate said, clearly familiar with this man. "So that it may be included on the record, you are here to defend Mr Walker?"

"Indeed." Mr Blackthorne smiled a small, quiet sort of smile and cast a look over at Lucas.

He was familiar, Lucas thought, but from where? When?

The justice gave a dismissive wave of his hand, much to the apparent chagrin of the prosecutor and the glaring officers. Mr Blackthorne folded his hands behind his back.

The proceedings began and passed in a blur. Sergeant Kahn and the sandy-haired constable—one Mr Gable—attested to his crimes and that they'd arrested him outside the cemetery. They'd got the tip from a reliable informant, they said, who'd requested to remain anonymous.

When it came time for the justices of the peace to hear Lucas's defence, they turned to him.

"Mr Blackthorne, if you or your client have anything to say to the court, now would be your opportunity."

Lucas looked to the justices. Not a damned word that came out of his mouth would change their minds. Was there even a point to saying that the officers and Pendleton were lying? For that matter, what would Blackthorne say that could possibly help? Lucas wished they'd had even a few moments before all this to speak.

But Blackthorne took a step forward, away from Lucas, all easy grace and seemingly unbothered by anything that had thus far transpired.

"Good day, gentlemen of the most distinguished court. You've already heard the stories of Sergeant Kahn and Constable Gable, and I would now like to set the record straight, if I may, to clear the good name of my client."

The second magistrate sniffed. "Stories? Are you saying our law enforcement was *lying* about him thieving?"

"I'm saying," Blackthorne said patiently, "that they fabricated the entire thing, yes. Mr Walker was not present at the graveyard at all."

Lucas's expression fell. What in the world was this man trying to do? Maybe a good lawyer could have convinced the court he'd not stolen anything, but to convince them he'd not been there *at all?* Blackthorne was mad!

"You see, Mr Walker here *was* arrested, however he was not in the process of stealing anything, and certainly not amid the desecration of any grave. Mr Walker was otherwise occupied the night of the twenty-seventh of December."

Blackthorne placed a comforting hand upon Lucas's shoulder. "What he is guilty of, if anything, was crossing the path of one Mr Alan Pendleton, who has been a known informant of the police for the last year—and who has pointed the finger at three other men for crimes they did not commit and who were later cleared of all charges."

"And why would an informant do such a thing?" the prosecutor scoffed.

"Men will say many untrue things when the police are paying them," Blackthorne said, and the magistrates murmured amongst themselves.

The prosecutor sputtered. "Asinine! And insulting, to boot, to say that our esteemed law enforcement would do such a thing."

"It wouldn't be the first time. I have examples, if you'd like to hear them, Mr Burbery?"

"Not necessary!" Burbery, the prosecutor, looked ready to pop a vein in his forehead.

The second magistrate looked to Lucas even as Blackthorne approached to offer out a few sheets of paper, perhaps containing the aforementioned examples. "Mr Walker, is what your advocate says true?"

Lucas's heart lodged itself in his throat. If he lied now, he'd be guilty of perjury. But if he denied it, he'd find himself in jail—and the credibility of his attorney in the gutter. He swallowed hard, his voice weak. "Yes, sir."

"All of this is hearsay, Your Honour!" Burbery bellowed. "If the defence has no proof, then all this is a ploy for a thief to walk away freely."

"Ah, yes." Blackthorne turned towards the back of the room, which Lucas had not had a chance to look at much. "Miss McCormick, would you come forward, please?"

McCormick? Lucas frowned, looking askance, his jaw just about dropping when he saw Madeline from The Sun and Stars strolling up alongside Blackthorne. She looked out of place there, awkward, her hands wrung together.

Blackthorne turned to address the justices once more. "This is Miss Madeline McCormick. She so happens to be a working woman at The Sun and Stars near Whitechapel and a witness to Mr Walker's whereabouts the night the police allegedly found him grave robbing. Is that correct, ma'am?"

" 'Tis, sir, aye." Madeline didn't seem to know where her eyes should be, so she stared at Blackthorne. "Mr Walker is an occasional visitor. He was there that night, from nine 'til midnight or thereabouts."

"In your company, Miss?" the first magistrate asked, arching a brow. No doubt every bloke in the room was eyeing Madeline with interest and every woman in disdain, and Lucas's heart hurt for her. She'd always been a kind girl, sharp-tongued and bright. Why she was lying for him, he didn't begin to understand.

"In my company," Madeline agreed.

"May I ask what the two of you were doing?"

"Each other, really." The court erupted into a mixture of nervous laughter and disgusted sounds, but Madeline gave a cheeky smile. "D'you need more details, sirs?"

The justices exchanged uncomfortable looks. One of them coughed. "That won't be necessary, no. Can anyone else back up your claim?"

"I can."

Lucas's eyes widened. He did turn then, enough that he spotted Jasper amongst the crowd.

And beside him, Henry Glass.

Christ almighty, I'm dreaming. This is all some wild, loony dream. He braced his hands against the table before him, dizzy. He didn't spot Barker in the crowd, but he supposed it would be dangerous for the other man to show up—but now Lucas realised where he knew Blackthorne from. He was the bloke at The Rusty Duck that night, the one Barker had been eyeing from across the room.

The one, Lucas realised now, Henry and Barker had been speaking to. The one Lucas had got himself all worked up over.

Jasper kept close to Glass's side. He was dressed so neatly, his hair tied back, looking more like a gentleman than Lucas had ever seen. His hands were clasped before himself, knuckles mottled white with his tight grip, and his voice shook when he tried to project it to the courtroom. "My name is Jasper Rees. I saw Mr Walker and his companion, Mr Barker, come and go at the hours Miss McCormick stated."

"As did I," Glass then added, voice smooth and easy, unflinchingly convincing in its lie. "My name is Henry Glass. I'm a surgeon at St. Mary's. I encountered Mr Walker and Mr Daniel Barker as they were leaving. We've met before, and we stopped to chat a bit on the street."

"Mr Barker," Blackthorne added, "also appears to have a warrant for his arrest for the same charges."

Lucas gawked at his friends. Four people were now lying on his behalf—committing perjury—and Glass in particular was risking far too much to do it. Even the suggestion that he was the sort of man to visit a place like The Sun and Stars would be prime gossip material. Lucas's stomach rolled at the thought.

The prosecutor looked between them all with a frustrated scowl. He could have asked them questions, Lucas thought, but they'd caught him off guard and he seemed at a loss. He finally shook his head and squared his shoulders, recovering. "I feel it pertinent to add that Mr Walker has previously been arrested for inciting violence at his former place of employment. It should attest to his poor character."

Blackthorne turned to address the magistrates, hands in his pockets, voice calm, unruffled. "As you can see, gentlemen, we have three witnesses—one a *very* credible gentleman—who are in agreement as to Mr Walker's whereabouts the night of the allegations. And yet the police have not produced a single witness beyond themselves, not even their informant who, as previously mentioned, is severely lacking in the credibility department.

"It's true that Mr Walker was previously charged with inciting a riot, a charge which he was later cleared of, I should add. What Mr Burbery is not telling you is that this so-called 'riot' was a strike Mr Walker organised at his place of employment, protesting the miserable working conditions and wages." Blackthorne turned to Lucas then, giving him a smile that was both kind and sincere. "Last I heard, wanting better for yourself and your fellow man was not a crime. That will be all."

He did not take a seat. No one did. There was little point; trials went so swiftly, and this one had already run longer than anyone seemed to care for—Lucas included. The justices leaned in to one another, murmuring amongst themselves.

There were three possible outcomes to this event. The justices could deem this something out of their scope and move it along to a quarter session to be reviewed by a judge and jury, they could convict and sentence him themselves, or…they could let him go. All Lucas could do was wait, breath caught in his chest.

And when they pronounced him not guilty and dismissed him from the courtroom, Lucas nearly cried out in joy.

TWENTY-NINE

He waited until they were all outside on the street before acknowledging his friends, though no sooner had he stepped onto the sidewalk than Jasper flung his arms around Lucas's neck and hugged him tight with a delighted laugh. Lucas in turn squeezed him around the middle and spun him in a full circle, eyes welling with tears.

"How in the world... All of you..." Lucas couldn't find the words. The gratefulness swelled in his chest and made his tongue feel two sizes too large, unable to formulate a coherent sentence.

"We should have this conversation elsewhere," Mr Blackthorne interrupted. "Shall we reconvene and have a chat? I'm sure Mr Walker has questions."

A ton of them, Lucas thought.

He looked over to Henry, who had not stopped smiling since they stepped outside and who offered, "Back to my place, if that suits everyone fine. Supper, drinks?"

"I should probably be heading back," Madeline began, but Jasper caught her by the hand and smiled broadly.

"Won't you come with us? We owe you."

She seemed to consider that, gaze flickering nervously about the lot of them, but then she relaxed and smiled a bit. "Oh, all right."

They split up, with Henry and Blackthorne taking one carriage and Lucas crawling into another with Jasper and Madeline. Jasper kept close to his side, looping their arms together once they were seated. That clinginess was a testament to how worried he'd been. Lucas couldn't blame him. He himself was still fending off the overwhelming nausea that had flooded him for the last few weeks. Now that everything was over and done with, it felt like a dam had been broken, and he wanted to sleep and cry and laugh all at once.

"You're both incredible," Lucas said in the privacy of the cab. "Just fuckin' incredible. How did all of this even come about?"

Jasper tipped his chin back to look at him. "After you were arrested, Mr Barker went straightaway to Mr Glass to tell him what had happened. Barker came to me a few days later. We lost track of you for a bit; Sergeant Kahn wouldn't tell me where they'd taken you."

Lucas gave him an apologetic look. "I shoulda written. I was just worried about gettin' you lot in trouble. How'd you figure out where I was?"

Jasper shook his head. "Mr Blackthorne stepped in. He and Mr Glass are acquaintances, and Blackthorne offered to help. Once he showed up at Kahn's door, they buckled pretty quickly and told us where you'd been taken. You received his letter?"

"Yeah, coupl'a days ago." Lucas rolled his shoulders back; they were aching and stiff from weeks of sleeping on that uncomfortable wooden plank of a bed. "So, you all thought lying would be the best form of clearing my name, huh."

Madeline sniffed indignantly. "That was not our first plan, no. But Mr Barker encountered that Pendleton bloke and had a few words with him."

Lucas's eyebrows rose. "Really?"

"At The Duck," Jasper confirmed. "Barker cornered him and got out of him what exactly he'd divulged to the police."

"He told them I'm a sodomite," Lucas responded sourly.

"We know." Jasper's lashes lowered. "We were concerned going with the truth would work against us if they decided to throw that little fact out to the magistrates."

"Even if they ain't got proof, once they heard it, they wouldn't just un-hear it," Madeline said solemnly.

Lucas looked at her. "How'd you get involved, then?"

She shrugged. "Jasper asked. Given that he got a good beating from that bloke who tried to hurt me a few months back, I felt I owed it to him. Besides, I rather like your face. Seemed a shame for you not to be comin' around anymore. Maybe it was seeing Mr Glass, too. Never seen a man so worried for someone before."

His pulse kicked up, fingers twitching where they rested against Jasper's arm. "He was awfully worried, was he?"

"Mr Barker said he'd never seen him so distraught," Jasper said gently, not without a knowing smile in Lucas's direction. "He helped to put this plan together, I should add. Got us all to correlate our stories. I suppose you owe him a thank you."

Lucas couldn't help a crooked grin. "You have no idea."

THIRTY

They arrived shortly after Henry and Blackthorne, but already Frederick and the cook had food out on the table. It was short notice for a proper, full-course meal, but there was no shortage of sandwiches, desserts, breads, biscuits, and soup. More important than that, when Lucas entered, Barker rose to his feet abruptly and hurried over with his eyes wide.

Lucas laughed. "You look like you're gonna hug me, mate."

Barker stopped in front of him and smiled, just a little, but it was still significantly more than he normally permitted past that sour face of his. Instead of a hug, he lifted a hand, offering a familiar-looking item to Lucas.

His eyes widened. His cap! He took it and clutched it to his chest.

Barker waved him off. "Don't get emotional on me, Walker. You've just got the devil's own luck."

"Nah, just some really great people in my life." He spared a glance towards Glass, who had taken up his seat at the head of the table.

They all sat and tucked into their impromptu supper and drinks. They regaled Lucas in greater detail with what had transpired in his absence, about how Barker—who had indeed been faking his fit that night—had come pounding on Glass's door in a panic.

The following few days, they'd tried to determine the best course of action. Barker couldn't go to the police to ask questions because they would have arrested him. Glass couldn't do it because they might have looked too closely at him and why he was associated with someone of Lucas's status and then pinpoint who Lucas had been stealing bodies for. Barker came up with the idea of seeking Jasper, who had been out of his mind with worry.

Not that the police had offered much information to Jasper. They'd brushed him off again and again, although he went nearly every day inquiring about Lucas's court date, his whereabouts, how Jasper might get a letter to him.

Jasper took great joy in speaking about Barker's encounter with Pendleton, despite not having personally witnessed it. Lucas's only regret was that he couldn't have been there to see it either, nor to knock the bastard's teeth in. Pendleton had never seemed too fond of Lucas. Or Barker, for that matter. But that last bit—it stung something fierce. Pendleton was like them, so to sell them out based on their affinity for men seemed particularly treacherous.

"What ended up happening to Pendleton?" Lucas asked.

"I told him to get out of the city, so if he knows what's good for him, that's what he did," Barker said.

"I would've loved to have been there to see all that."

"As would I," Henry added.

Lucas stole a look across the table at him with a small smile. Henry had been very quiet so far this evening, allowing everyone else to do the talking. His expression remained largely unreadable throughout it all.

Jasper went on to say that Henry had sought out Theseus Blackthorne, who had been more than happy to offer his assistance—free of charge, even, which had Lucas eyeing the man with suspicion as to why he'd be so willing to do such a thing for Henry unless he had some ulterior motive. Lucas also noted how, just like at the pub, Barker couldn't seem to keep his eyes off the lawyer, except when Blackthorne looked his way and Barker swiftly dropped his gaze to stare at anything but him.

Blackthorne and Henry had conjured up the story for them to tell and determined one more witness besides Jasper would be beneficial—someone to state they were directly with Lucas at the time he was supposedly breaking into the cemetery. Madeline had provided that. Henry had been their safeguard, however; a gentleman's word was worth far more than that of two prostitutes and even that of the officers.

As the night wound down, the energy of the group began to subside, replaced with exhaustion from the day's events. Blackthorne offered to take Barker home, and Lucas caught the latter's eye and wiggled his eyebrows, at which Barker promptly gave a staunch middle finger. Jasper and Madeline caught another cab to head home as well, leaving Lucas alone with Henry.

Finally. Not that he hadn't been thrilled for their company, but some part of him had been eager to get Henry to himself. He remained in the parlour while Henry saw the others out, petting Hilda, who had settled in his lap. When the other man returned and had a seat, the pair lingered in silence for a few moments, enjoying the calmness and stillness of the room.

Frederick eventually entered. "I thought Master Walker might like a bath after his gruelling last few weeks."

Lucas dropped his head back and sighed. If there was one thing that would entice him away from Henry right now... "God, yes, please."

Frederick saw to it that the tub was filled, and Lucas gladly languished in the hot water until every inch of himself was scrubbed clean and smelled of soap. By the time he drained the water and got out, the house was mostly dark and quiet, Frederick likely having gone to bed and Henry seeming to have retired upstairs for the night. Lucas half expected to be going straight to his guest room, but when he ascended the stairs, Henry's bedchamber door opened and the man looked out into the hall.

Their eyes met. It was as much of an invitation as Lucas needed, really.

He stepped into Henry's rooms for the first time, thinking how peculiar it was to do so in a nightgown and with his hair a mess sticking up in all directions. Something Henry remedied when, a moment later, he reached out to card his fingers back through the wet strands and smooth them down. The sudden gesture of affection made Lucas go still, worried if he moved, it might frighten Henry away.

Instead they stood there in the centre of the bedchamber, Lucas in his nightgown, Henry still in his trousers and shirt, but having previously discarded every other part of his attire.

Lucas forced his mouth to cooperate with him. "You've been awfully quiet tonight."

"Everyone else seemed to do plenty of talking," Henry murmured, again combing his fingers through Lucas's hair, brushing it from his face. "I assumed I would have my chance to speak with you once they'd had their say."

Lucas swallowed thickly. "I owe you a really big debt of gratitude."

"You owe me nothing, Lucas. Everything that happened, happened because you were working for me."

"You should do that more often," Lucas murmured, distracted.

Henry chuckled. "Blame myself? Or touch your hair?"

"Well, hair touchin's nice, too. But I meant you callin' me by my name."

The surgeon's expression went all soft and adoring around the edges. He drifted closer to Lucas, and his hands lifted again, warm palms cupping the sides of Lucas's face as though he were something delicate and treasured. "Lucas."

Oh, Lord, there was something about the way his name sounded on Henry's lips that made his knees weak every damned time. He closed his eyes, breathed deep, and pressed his cheek against one of those hands. It seemed only fair that, if Henry was going with his Christian name, he ought to do the same. "Henry."

Speaking it aloud was a spark igniting and illuminating a dark room. Henry let out a soft, wanting sound and closed the distance between them. It was not the first time they'd kissed, of course, but it was the first time that *Henry* had kissed *him*, and that flooded Lucas with excitement. He straightened up and slanted their mouths together, all sinewy eagerness and heat.

Lucas's hands sought out the fastens on Henry's trousers, thinking back to the evening they'd kissed in the cellar, how he'd felt Henry's stiff cock pressed up against him and how badly he'd wanted to get on his knees for the man. Lucas had a feeling, given Henry's shyness, it had been some time since he'd let anyone touch him in any fashion.

Trousers contended with, Lucas dragged them down Henry's hips while Henry drew back just enough to make quick work of his shirt, and they did not stop until every article of clothing—including Lucas's nightclothes—had been discarded.

Henry kissed him again, the taste of brandy still on his tongue as it slipped past Lucas's lips, coaxing a moan from his throat. Lucas took a step forward, prodding Henry back and to the bed, where Lucas disengaged from the kiss to shove Henry onto the mattress, cast him a cheeky grin, and crawl on top of him to straddle his hips.

For the first time, Lucas was able simply to take a moment to look and appreciate every sharp angle and line of Henry's body, and the way his skin felt when Lucas braced his hands against the other man's chest, the rise and fall of it with each breath. The slight twitch of his mouth, nervous but hopeful, and the way his eyes raked over every inch of Lucas as though to devour him whole with but a look all made Lucas's pulse race.

"You're beautiful," Henry breathed, lifting a hand to brush the backs of his fingers along Lucas's jaw. "I thought so from the moment I laid eyes on you."

Lucas grinned, shifting atop him, savouring the hitch of Henry's breath as he did so. "Propositioning you in a dark alley?"

"Propositioning me in a dark alley," Henry agreed with quiet amusement. Then, to Lucas's surprise, Henry jerked upward and caught him around the middle, flipping them over to put Lucas beneath him and settling between his thighs. "I wonder how much differently things would have gone if I'd taken you up on it."

Lucas's heart damned near skipped a beat, and his previously half-hard cock immediately stood to full attention. "Not too late to take me up on it now."

Henry smiled in that soft, patient way of his. He bowed over Lucas but rather than kiss his mouth, Henry brought his lips to the younger man's jaw, then up to his ear, the spot just beneath it... Every featherlight touch made Lucas's skin prickle in delight, especially as those lips began to move south. They took in the long line of exposed flesh, his neck, the hollow of his throat, down to his chest. And then Henry travelled further south, and the moment he descended below Lucas's navel, Lucas drew in a breath and held it.

Then Henry's mouth wrapped around his cock, and Lucas saw stars.

He dropped his head back, muscles all along his stomach contracting, pulling tight, as he tried to refrain from bucking his hips up into that lovely, wet heat. Henry's tongue stroked along the underside of Lucas's prick before drawing off him almost completely, sucking on the head of him. Lucas was all too aware they weren't alone in the house, and for that reason only, he bit down on his lip, fighting back the moan that wanted to let loose from his throat. It had been so long since anyone had touched him—or even since he'd touched himself. Prison had hardly granted him privacy for such things.

But this, he thought, was most definitely worth the wait.

Tension built like a storm, slow and steady. Lucas's fingers found their way into Henry's hair, twisting into the soft brown waves, mussing up their carefully constructed style. Henry's lips and cheeks and tongue working along his shaft coaxed him eagerly to the edge until his breath came in short, laboured pants and he could focus on little else beyond fucking the heat of that delicious mouth and the urge to come inside of it.

The moment that blissful end came near...Henry pulled off his cock.

Lucas whimpered in protest and opened his eyes to gaze down at the older man with a hundred different curses on the tip of his tongue. "Fuck..."

Henry rocked back, tongue swiping across his pinkened lips and cutting a smile that made Lucas's insides flutter. "I'd be terribly remiss if I gave you what you wanted so easily."

"You're an arse," Lucas groaned, rolling his hips up, as fruitless a gesture as it was.

"I would agree with that." Henry's fingers ghosted across the tip of his saliva-slicked cock, down the underside of it, dipping between his thighs and cupping his sac with the utmost gentleness. "Tell me what you'd like."

Lucas's mind blanked. What did he want? He wanted Henry's mouth on him again. He wanted Henry inside of him. He wanted to be inside of Henry. At that exact moment, feeling Henry's fingers cradling him like that, he would have settled for a quick jerk, to be honest. He wanted *everything*.

He wet his lips. "C'mere."

Henry gave him a quizzical look but obediently moved back up his body. No sooner had he done so did Lucas grab him around the middle, dragging Henry atop him until their legs were intertwined and their bodies aligned. Stomach to stomach, hip to hip, cock to cock. As Henry's eyes fluttered closed, Lucas gave a purposeful jerk of his pelvis, grinding up against him.

That was good, Lucas decided. He gripped Henry's waist, sliding their erections together, trapped between the warmth of both their bodies with just enough friction to drag Lucas right back to the edge of release.

At that edge was where he tried to remain, coasting along the brim of orgasm and savouring the feel of Henry's body, the sound of his laboured breathing and the occasional strangled gasp. He found himself so focused on Henry and how bloody beautiful he was that Lucas didn't give a care to himself.

And when he slid a hand to cup Henry's cheek tenderly in his palm, kissed his mouth, and breathed, "I want to hear you," Henry let out a startled, desperate moan and bucked down once more. The warmth of his release against Lucas's stomach made him shudder, unable to help a jerk of his own hips even as Henry bowed his head to Lucas's shoulder and tried to catch his breath.

Lucas wove his fingers into Henry's hair, holding him near while they both relearned how to breathe. It was a chore to be still. He had half a mind to shove a hand down and finish himself off, but patience was a virtue. Waiting would be worth it.

Henry drew a few lazy kisses across his throat and up to his jaw, each one carefully placed and lovingly doled out. He murmured fondly, "How am I ever going to keep up with the likes of you?"

"Do your best?" Lucas grinned despite himself, head tipped back to bare more of his throat, granting Henry all the access he wanted to it. "Though if you don't touch me soon, I might just have to throw myself into a cold bath."

He punctuated this sentiment with a tug at Henry's hair and a lift of his own hips so that his still-hardened prick pressed against Henry's stomach.

Henry flashed him a wry smile and, just as Lucas had hoped that he would, scaled his way back down Lucas's body. The messy remnants of his own spend didn't seem to bother him in the slightest as he sucked the head of Lucas's cock back into his mouth, laving his tongue across the tip in a way that made Lucas fall apart a little inside. *Could Henry taste himself?* Holding that thought for longer than a moment was not possible, not when Henry continued to take more of Lucas past his lips, both too gentle and too overwhelming at the same time.

Lucas sank back into the mattress, forcing himself to relax completely. He carded his fingers through Henry's hair, cradled the back of his head, and refrained from jerking into his mouth every time Henry drew off and only took him back in torturously slowly. The easy, languid pace was delightful in and of itself. There was nothing hurried about Henry's actions, and Lucas wanted to drag out their pleasure, to enjoy every minuscule inch of build-up that soon had him panting and his muscles quivering.

Henry's fingers, previously wrapped around the base of his cock, drew away then, damp with saliva, to dip lower, and reflex had Lucas parting his legs, biting down on his lip in hopeful anticipation. When Henry slid two fingers inside of him, they went in slow and easy, and the bright sting of pain faded swiftly.

His fingers curled, probed, pressed in deep, and that slow-building storm bubbled right over. Lucas clutched at Henry's hair and let out a sharp cry, coming hard, spilling himself into the other man's mouth. Everything in the world ceased to matter beyond *Henry, Henry, Henry*, and that was *glorious*.

Henry worked him until he began to soften. When Henry drew back, it was with a quiet cough and a discreet hand across his mouth, but the absence of him made Lucas bite out a plaintive whimper. At least until Henry moved upward to stretch out alongside him, fingertips trailing up Lucas's side, picking across his ribs and over his chest. *Skilled surgeon's hands*, Lucas thought. Hands that had saved countless lives.

He was beginning to think his own life was one of them.

THIRTY-ONE

Lucas slept well past noon the next day. An empty bed was the only greeting when he woke but given the time on the clock above the mantel, he suspected that was all well and good. Henry was likely at work or puttering about the house.

Lucas took his time before crawling out of bed, sleepy-eyed but with a lightness to his movements he hadn't felt in…hell, far longer than he could recall.

Frederick saw to his lunch for him, and he had another bath, just because he could. As he'd thought, Henry had left for work early that morning, which sparked an inkling of guilt that Lucas had kept him up so late the night before.

Being (mostly) alone in Henry Glass's house for the day might have been boring for some, but it was an adventure for Lucas. He had afternoon tea in the parlour with Frederick, insisting the man have a seat and chat with him a bit. Afterwards, he thumbed through the various tomes on the shelves, mostly medical texts, all far above Lucas's understanding but fascinating all the same. Later, Frederick directed him to the guest room where, Lucas discovered, all of his meagre belongings from his flat had been brought. Knowing his rent wouldn't get paid, Jasper had taken it upon himself to get in there, gathering the fine clothing Henry had bought for him along with some of the other things he owned.

That afternoon, he napped in Henry's large, luxurious bed. This time he woke to a hand in his hair, stroking it back from his face, and he opened his eyes to Henry seated on the mattress beside him and giving him the loveliest smile Lucas had ever seen.

"You're home," Lucas said.

"You stayed," Henry replied, sounding awed.

"Did you think I wouldn't?"

"I don't know." Henry paused, then leaned down to kiss him warmly on the mouth. "I feared you wouldn't, I suppose."

"Why?"

Another pause as Henry sat up, back to the headboard beside him. "We hadn't spoken much about…any of this. We made no commitments. I suppose I wasn't sure where things stood."

Lucas shifted, laying himself in Henry's lap so that he could encourage the man to pet his hair, which he began to do without hesitation. "I get the no close relationships thing, but I've gathered you ain't much for takin' people to bed on a whim, neither."

"You would be correct."

"There a reason for that?"

Henry sighed, tipping his head back to stare at the ceiling. "Many reasons, I suppose. Shame might be a part of it. Fear might be another."

"What are you afraid of?" Lucas asked.

"Rejection. Ridicule. When you spend your life hiding such an important part of yourself, worrying what it might do to your family name, your career… It's a daunting thing to allow anyone else to see that part of you." Henry looked down again, and his smile was sad. "Maybe that's why I've reached out how I have, trying to help others within our little community. Making friends. It was a safer way for me to be honest about myself."

Henry was a man who seemed so confident in his trade and in his everyday dealings with others. Yet Lucas had seen the hesitation and timidness in Henry's dealings with him, which was why it had confused him so much.

He lifted a hand to touch Henry's jaw. "And are we past all that now? You pulling away, making choices for me?"

Henry lowered his lashes. "I cannot promise my insecurities won't get the better of me from time to time, but I'm trying."

"What on earth would you have to be insecure about?"

"Plenty, I should think. You are attractive and engaging. And very much… not the sort of man I thought would have any lasting interest in someone like me."

That statement brought a laugh bubbling from Lucas's chest. "*Me* not be interested in *you*? Are you daft?" When Henry frowned, Lucas gave his head a shake. "I'm some poor kid from Whitechapel. I grew up chasing rats in the sewers. I haven't got a damned thing to offer anyone—let alone someone as brilliant as you."

"I think you sorely underestimate yourself, Lucas." Henry's hand stilled in his hair for a moment. "Blackthorne mentioned about your job at Whitaker's… the strike. Will you tell me about it?"

Lucas grimaced. "Not sure what there is to tell. We were all exhausted, bein' made to work long hours, skipping meals, constantly getting hurt on malfunctioning machinery. I just wanted them to start treatin' us right, you know? So, I got a bunch of the other lads to agree to go on strike 'til the bosses caved and agreed to compromise with us."

The memory was still so fresh, the excitement he'd felt at doing something *good* and *right*. The idea that those men, most of whom were supporting families, deserved something better than what they were getting had spurred him on, hungry for change.

Lucas had been so tired of being looked down on, of being treated as lesser, just because his family had been poor.

"And I take it that things did not go according to plan."

"Rarely do, do they?" Lucas sighed, fixing his gaze upon the ceiling.

"Everyone was on board at first. Then, some people gave up. Said they couldn't afford to go without—that meagre wages was better than nothin'. We were all trying to support one another, helpin' out those who were struggling the most, but it wasn't enough, I guess. They started dropping like flies.

"In the end, it was just twenty or so of us, makin' as much noise as we could. We stormed the factory one mornin', demanding to speak with the owner himself. Things got...a little violent, I guess. His men got in our faces, we got in theirs, a fight broke out. Me and a few others got arrested, and every one of 'em threw me to the wolves and said I'd instigated the entire thing."

It had been a betrayal of the sharpest kind. Lucas had so badly wanted to help improve their lives, and they'd seemed all for it—until they weren't. Up until they'd become more concerned with saving their own necks.

After that, work had become impossible to find. The owners of factories in the area had talked, and then most had known Lucas by name and, soon enough, by sight. A few times he'd thought he'd got lucky by landing a new job, only to be found out a few weeks later and thrown to the streets. His work ethic had not mattered. The fact that he'd lost his home, that he'd been going hungry, had not mattered. He'd posed a threat, and they'd reacted accordingly.

A touch to his jaw coaxed him back to the present. He found himself gazing up at Henry's concerned face, feeling warm fingertips stroke along his skin. "It's unfortunate that not so many men in the world have the compassionate heart that you do."

A compassionate heart... Was that what it was? Jasper had always told him he was a good man, but Jasper saw the best in everyone, even when he shouldn't. Henry was at least a little more practical in the way he saw people. "I'll take your word on that."

"Good. You should."

Lucas reached up, touching a hand to his cheek once more. "What comes next, Henry? For us, I mean."

Henry turned his head, pressing a kiss into Lucas's palm. "I suppose that largely depends on you."

"You still need me 'n' Barker to bring you bodies, don't you?"

"I've been thinking a lot about that, actually." With a sigh, Henry leaned back. "I think…my days of hiring grave robbers are almost at an end."

Lucas's chest cinched tight in worry. "Why?"

"Because this was too close. Had you or Barker been seriously punished because of me, I'd never have forgiven myself. The both of you are too important."

He could have argued. He could have pointed out that they'd been doing this for months—Barker for years—and only been caught once, and it had been due to outside influence. But Lucas had no interest in guilting Henry into anything. Whatever that meant for Barker and himself, they'd have to figure it out. Henry Glass was not responsible for their financial well-being.

"What will you do for research, then?"

"There's been talk of a new form of embalming. I've yet to try it, but if a proven method of preserving a cadaver has presented itself, then I'd be a fool not to take advantage of it. Finding a body through legal means every few months is significantly easier than every few days, and I would have far more time to perform my research before the cadaver began to decay."

Fair enough, Lucas thought. "That sounds grand."

"As for you…" Henry looked down at him again. "I'm uncertain how well you'll take to my suggestion."

That didn't bode well, did it? "Let's hear it, then."

Henry took a deep breath, seeming to steady his nerves. "Move in here. With me."

Lucas stilled, then pushed himself up to sitting, twisting around to face him. "Move in here."

A hundred different emotions played across Henry's face: worry, uncertainty, hopefulness among them. He wrung his hands together, staring down at them. "I know you dislike the idea of anyone looking after you, but it would be a logical step, mutually beneficial. Everyone in my employ is aware of our leanings, so within these walls, we needn't keep anything a secret. To the rest of the world, you would be...I don't know. I would tell them you were a member of my staff, I suppose; we'd figure something out..."

He was rambling, and it was quite possibly the most adorable thing Lucas had seen.

But...moving in here, with Henry? The thought made his mind spin. What would he do with his time? He could, perhaps, look for employment somewhere or find some way to make himself useful to Henry, body-snatching aside.

Beyond all that, though, Lucas saw the offer for what it was: commitment. A promise that Henry would no longer be holding him at arm's length. The walls of Henry's castle were finally coming down.

Lucas smiled wide, a laugh wanting to burst free. "Yeah, all right."

Henry stopped, gaze flicking up to him, startled. Clearly, he'd so heavily anticipated Lucas saying *no* that he'd not stopped to consider that he just might say *yes*. "All right? Yes?"

"S'what I said."

"Oh. Well." Henry paused, a silly little smile pulling at his mouth. "Wonderful."

Lucas did laugh then, scooting forward to settle himself into Henry's lap, taking the older man's face in his hands.

"Wonderful," he agreed and pressed a warm kiss to Henry's mouth. "Took you long enough to accept my proposition, Mr Glass, but I suppose some things are worth the wait."

ALSO BY KELLEY

AS K. YORK
Unchained
Glass Castles (The Resurrectionists Book 1)
Dark Horse (The Resurrectionists Book 2)

AS KELLEY YORK
The *Dark is the Night* series:
A Light Amongst Shadows
A Hymn in the Silence
A Calm Before the Storm
A Shimmer in the Night
The Wrath of Wolves

STANDALONES
Into the Glittering Dark
Dirty London
Suicide Watch
Modern Monsters
Made of Stars
Other Breakable Things
Hushed

9 781960 322081